I0582018

CLAIMED BY *Her Bear*

THE MONTANA GRIZZLIES 2

ARIEL MARIE

A grizzly bear who desired one thing she hadn't yet found in life. One scent changed everything.

Pola Prime was a shifter who wanted to find her fated mate. Watching her sister claim hers left Pola feeling a little jealous. She kept hope alive that she would be next. There was a woman out there for her. She just had to find her.

A night on the town revealed a wonderful surprise.

Her mate.

Shekita Harper wanted to avoid relationships and just have a little fun. Thanks to her ex, she had a fear of possessive women. She was her own person and didn't want to belong to anyone.

But then she met Pola, a bear shifter who was beautiful and funny and wanted to claim her.

Pola didn't want to risk losing Shekita, so she would give her time. She'd woo her mate and get her to love her.

Pola hoped she was enough for Shekita to forget her past and move toward a future with her.

If you love steamy, sapphic paranormal romance with a possessive bear shifter and her beautiful human mate, then you will enjoy Claimed by Her Bear. This story was intended for mature readers only.

***Please note, Claimed by Her Bear was featured in the Flirting With Darkness anthology. It has now been released on its own.*

CHAPTER ONE

"Hello, my loving sister." Pola Prime walked into Dasha's backyard. She knew she would find her older sibling in the yard, painting. Dasha must not have heard her. Pola smiled and stood a few feet away from her, watching her work. She was so proud of her.

Dasha was an in-demand artist with a wild following. Her primary focus was nature, and each one of her paintings were unique. Her arms moved with bold strokes while the painting came to life before her.

Pola cleared her throat again.

"Dasha," she called out in a singsong voice.

Dasha jumped, her head spinning around. A smile came to her face when she realized who was calling her name.

"Hey, Pola."

Dasha had always been the awkward, quiet sibling of the three of them. It was amazing how different three people who came from the same set of parents could be. Recently, there had been a change with Dasha. Her bear had recognized her mate, and she'd fallen in love.

With Pola's best friend, Saffron.

Imagine Pola's surprise that her sister and best friend would be fated mates. She didn't know how that had come to be. Dasha had always been grumpy toward Saffron when they were younger. Dasha was ten years older than Saffron and Pola. She'd never wanted to be bothered by the girls, but now Pola understood. It must have been Dasha's way of pushing Saffron away because deep down she was infatuated with the younger woman, but she didn't know it.

At first Pola was hurt. Only for a brief moment. Who was she to go against fate? She quickly embraced her best friend as her sister-in-law. She only had one rule that she had to set with Saffron.

A shudder rippled through her body. There was one thing she didn't need to know about Dasha, and that was how she performed in the bedroom.

"How's work coming for you?" Pola asked, moving to stand next to Dasha. Her gaze swept the canvas, and Pola was proud of Dasha. The work was amazing. It was a picture of the lake Saffron's house sat beside. "Are you doing this from memory?"

"Yeah. Since we decided to stay up here for a few weeks, I wanted to put some paintings of the lake up for sale. We spend enough time there that it's easy to remember." Dasha smiled sheepishly.

"You are amazing." Pola leaned over and gave her a one-armed hug. She pulled back and glanced at the house. "Your mate is here, isn't she?"

"She is. She was in the shower the last time I was indoors." Dasha dropped her brush in a cup, cleaning it off in the solution. "How's the new job coming along?"

"It's amazing. I'm learning so much." Pola smiled. She practically bounced on the heels of her feet thinking of her new place of employment. She'd been hired recently as a secretary to the alpha bear of their clan.

The Brown Claw clan was one of the oldest in

Montana. Eddie Fang was a tough woman who ran the Brown Claw with an iron-clad fist. She was well respected, and it was her family who'd founded their town and clan. The Fang and Pride families were close. It was an honor to work for Eddie. Pola loved her community, and being able to serve as a secretary for their alpha and help keep her organized was a joy.

"That's good. What did you and Saffron have planned for today?" Dasha was focused again on her painting. She was working on the sky, and if Pola wasn't watching her, she would have sworn this was a photograph. That's how real-life Dasha's work was.

"We're heading down to the shop to check on the progress."

Saffron owned an ice cream shop, the Lick or Bite, that had burned down over six months ago. A deranged bear had been stalking Saffron, and he wouldn't take no for an answer. He'd trapped Saffron in her freezer and set the building on fire. Luckily, that story had a happy ending.

"Hey, Pola." Saffron bounded out of the house. She jogged down the stairs and came over to them. She and Pola shared a quick hug. "I'm ready."

"I was wondering if I'd told you what time I'd

be here. I was beginning to think you forgot." Pola chuckled.

"Nope. I'm all ready. I was on the phone with the contractor. He says they are ahead of schedule and the shop might be done earlier than we anticipated," Saffron said.

Her eyes drifted over to Dasha who must have felt her gaze. Their eyes connected, and a deep flush spread along Saffron's face. Dasha set her brush down and held open her arms. Saffron flew into them immediately.

Pola groaned and rolled her eyes. One would think after being mated for six months, they could keep their hands off each other. She spun around with a laugh and moved toward the front.

"I'll be in the car while you say goodbye," she called out over her shoulder. She made the mistake of looking and found Saffron and Dasha in the midst of a passionate kiss.

They probably hadn't heard her.

Pola sighed and headed to her car. She hoped fate had a plan for her. Dasha was the first of the Prime siblings to get mated. Their brother, Jaco, was happily living the single life. She doubted he was ready to settle down. Pola, on the other hand, would love to find someone to cuddle up with on cold nights and spend the warm summer evenings out in the wild—preferably naked.

It didn't take Saffron long to join her in the car. She slid into the passenger seat, flushed, and her hair slightly askew.

"Okay, now I'm ready," Saffron announced.

"You might want to fix your hair." Pola giggled. She rolled down the windows slightly. It was a beautiful spring day, and she loved to have the fresh air flowing in through the windows. She also wasn't going to admit she could scent her friend's slight hint of arousal. Saffron would be mortified. Even though they had grown up together and Saffron was used to shifters, she would still be horrified that Pola could pick up her reaction to Dasha.

"Oh, goodness." Saffron pulled down the visor and fixed her thick hair.

Pola threw the car in gear and guided the vehicle down their long driveway. Dasha's cabin was located deep in the woods on the side of the mountain. Only few people knew exactly where she and Saffron lived. Dasha was a very private person and had the cabin built away from civilization.

It didn't take long for them to reach their destination. Pola slowed her car as she drove down the street looking for a parking spot. There were a few trucks parked out front of the Lick or Bite. A small sedan eased out of a spot, and Pola snagged it before anyone else could. They exited her car and strode down the sidewalk toward the shop.

The building, luckily enough, didn't have much structure damage. Her friend had poured her life savings into opening this business when she'd decided to move home. Pola was happy that she'd had insurance on the place so she could reopen. The ice cream shop had been a staple in their childhood. Pola could remember many times she'd begged her parents for money so she could go get ice cream.

"She looks great, doesn't she?"

"They do seem like they are ahead. I wouldn't have imagined they would have made such progress."

They arrived outside the front of the establishment. The windows were covered with brown paper, and the door was open with music blasting from inside.

"Come on in. Since we were starting from scratch, I made a few changes to the setup." Saffron waved her in.

Pola followed her into the store, immediately hit with the smell of fresh paint and wood. She grimaced at the sound of the machinery filling the air.

"When can you start moving things in?" she asked.

They walked through the storefront and headed toward the back.

"I'm going to wait until they finish. I'm still unsure how I want to decorate and what theme I'll have in here." Saffron leaned against the wall, studying the area where the men were working. "Would you go shopping with me?"

"Of course. Just let me know when. You know how much I love shopping." Pola rested against the opposite one and took in her friend. "So, tell me. How are you really doing being back here?"

Saffron stiffened for a moment, exhaling loudly. What had happened here had been traumatizing for her. Pola still couldn't believe she had almost lost her best friend.

"I'm okay. It was rough coming back here at first, but I'm not a quitter. This is my business. It's my baby, and I can't have my fear holding me back. What Bishop did was—"

"I know. You don't have to say any more." Pola took Saffron's hands in hers.

They had been close since they'd been in

elementary school, and there wasn't anything Pola wouldn't do for Saffron. Had she had the chance, her bear would have gone on the attack to defend her, but luckily enough, Dasha had been there.

"I didn't mean to make you upset."

"It's okay." Saffron wiped her eyes with the back of her hand. She barked a laugh. "I try not to think about it. But I promised Dasha I would take it one day at a time. That's sort of my excuse for asking you to come here with me, so I could have someone with me."

"Anytime. I don't mind stopping by if you need me." Pola rubbed Saffron's shoulder. She meant every word. They had been through so much together, and she wouldn't hesitate to be by her side. "So, those two handsome men over there working, are they single?"

This time, Saffron's laugh was genuine.

"Mike and Rudy are both happily married," Saffron said. She pushed off the wall. "Let me show you the rest of the place before you go."

"Are you sure you will be okay if I leave? I can call and—"

"No, I'll be fine. Dasha will be here later. I have a few errands that are within walking distance."

Pola nodded and shadowed Saffron around the

rest of the shop. She was really impressed with the work the company had done so far. The Lick and Bite was going to be a cool, hip ice cream shop that the town was going to love once again.

At least the scent of smoke was no longer lingering in the air. Pola trailed behind her friend, her gaze scanning the place. A few men were working on putting the plaster on the walls. The setup had changed. It almost appeared larger than before.

"Why does it seem bigger?" Pola asked.

"We pushed this wall back to give us more room out here. I want to have more tables for people to be able to sit. I figured in the winter we can have some events for the kids, offer hot cocoa. Things to get people out once the snow hits."

"Yeah, because we all know when it's negative thirty, we all crave ice cream," Pola teased. She walked behind the counter, chuckling.

"We sure do," Saffron replied haughtily. She breezed past Pola and waved for her to follow her. "You won't get an invite then."

"I'm kidding. I think it's a great idea. I can speak with the alpha and I'm sure we can share the dates to get community engagement. She would love that."

They arrived at Saffron's office doorway. Saffron spun around with a wide grin.

"Would you?"

"Of course. I'm sure you could do a weekly thing. We could get others involved. Like, the librarians could read stories, we could have Santa…"

"That's what I was thinking!" Saffron held up her hand for a high five.

Pola slapped it, happy her friend was bouncing back from her horrific experience in the shop.

"What do you think?" Saffron asked.

"Nice." Pola stepped inside the small office. The walls had paint, the floors were wood, and there was a beautiful wood table in the center. Pola strolled over to it, running her fingers along the smooth surface. "This desk is beautiful."

"Isn't it? It was custom-made by the contractor. She's amazing, and her brother owns the company."

Pola inhaled, loving the scent of the pine wood. She caught a hint of a floral aroma that didn't go with the desk. It reminded Pola of fresh wildflowers that she would find deep in the forest during the springtime. Her bear sat up, intrigued also. She wasn't sure where the smell came from. Saffron didn't have any flowers in her bare office.

Why was her bear interested in the scent? Pola pushed it aside and roamed the small area.

Pola soon left the shop after finishing the tour. She'd promised Saffron she would return after work. Today was a half a day for her, and she didn't mind picking up Saffron and going to look for decorations for her office. It was a nice day to go on the hunt for bargain trinkets. It would be fun, and maybe they could grab an early dinner. Pola was sure her sister would be in the same spot they had left her when they returned.

Pola hopped into her vehicle and headed toward her office. The only thing was, now that she'd had that scent in her nostrils, she couldn't stop thinking about it. The faint hint of arousal flared to life.

"I need to get laid," Pola mumbled. It had been a while since she had been with anyone. Maybe she needed a night on the town to find someone to scratch her itch. Shifters, especially bears, had considerable sexual appetites. She was sure she would be able to find someone to have some fun with. Settling back in her seat, she was satisfied with her decision. She couldn't call on Saffron to go with her. Now that she was a mated woman, she wouldn't be going out on the prowl.

But that wouldn't stop her from asking if Dasha and Saffron would want to go with her. She'd ask, and if she gave her sister the biggest puppy dog eyes she could muster, she was sure she could convince both of them to join her.

A song on the radio piqued her interest. She turned the music up and sang along with it. Tonight was going to be fun. It had been a while since she'd gone out with her sister. Having Saffron and Dasha with her, she was sure she would have a good time.

CHAPTER TWO

"You sure you don't want to come with us?" Mike asked for the third time.

He and Rudy leaned against the ice cream shop's counter and eyed her. They were finished for the day, and they wanted to go down to the local watering hole and grab a few drinks.

It had been a long day for Shekita Harper. They were coming along with renovating the Lick and Bite. This was her first job where her brother had put her in charge as the contractor to work with the owner. Troy, who owned Harper Construction, had been pushing for her to take more responsibilities with the family business. She had been content just working as a carpenter, but Troy wanted her to oversee this job so he could run the business and start another project.

This had been a good year for them. The business was flourishing, which helped keep her busy. She'd had a rough couple of years. She'd been involved with a woman who hadn't appreciated her. The relationship had turned sour two years ago, and she'd had to escape.

Shekita inhaled sharply, not wanting to think about her.

Bobbie Curtis was a woman who had wooed Shekita. Their relationship had started out almost perfect. She was kind, fun, sexy, and possessive. Everything Shekita thought she had wanted in a partner. After about a year of dating, there were slight changes in Bobbie that Shekita had ignored. She didn't want to think that her lover would do her any harm.

Bobbie's sexy possessiveness that had drawn Shekita to her, turned into a dark jealousy where rage became involved.

Shekita blinked, not wanting to go down memory lane. She was no longer under Bobbie's thumb. She'd broken free from that prison that had become her life.

"I don't know, guys. We have to—"

"Oh, come on, Shekita. You work too hard. You are putting us to shame." Rudy chuckled. He pushed his safety glasses to the top of his head and narrowed his gaze on her. Rudy had worked for her brother for years and was close friends with Troy. He was a goofball but a really hard grafter. "One drink."

Shekita glanced around. All eyes were on her. She was the only woman on this crew and she was in charge of them. None of them had any issues with a woman running a construction site. She was damn good at her job, and they knew it. Each of her men were the best at what they did, and it made her job easy.

"Fine. One drink." She sighed.

Their cheers and claps made her smile. She rolled her eyes at their silly antics. It would feel nice to relax and get out. It had been a while since she had gone out with them. They were a fantastic group of guys and they always tried to include her as one of them.

"Where are we going?" she asked.

"There's a local bar I heard that had great

drinks, big televisions, and some lovely food," Hector said. He ran a hand through his dark hair, pushing it back away from his face. He was a ladies' man, and from the twinkle in his eyes, he was looking to get into something or someone.

Most of them were from the next town over, Black Fish. The drive normally took her about forty-five minutes to get to Lurton from her home. It wasn't a bad drive, and luckily enough, they were working during decent weather. If the winter was upon them, she may utilize a local hotel due to the snow. Montana winters could be brutal, and it would just be safer to stay in a hotel while on a job.

"Sounds great. Let's clean up and then we can head out." She turned and went back into Saffron's office.

The woman who owned the shop was nice, and Shekita had heard rumors all the way over in Black Fish that some bear shifter had tried to burn her alive in her shop. A shiver went through Shekita. Her heart went out to the woman. It was never easy to get past trauma, but Saffron appeared to be okay. She smiled and had even fallen in love. Shekita had met Saffron's mate, Dasha, who was bear shifter. The look in Dasha's eye when she stared after Saffron made Shekita's heart skip a beat. She hoped to find someone who gazed at her like that.

As if their entire world was centered around her.

In just few moments she had spent around the couple, it had given her faith that one day she would have that. Even though she was human, she believed in fate. There was someone out there for her. She just had to be patient.

But patience wasn't one of Shekita's strong suits.

She wanted a forever with someone.

The crew got to work tidying up the site. She had a firm rule that they had to have their workspaces clean and organized when they shut down. She had started working on a custom-built shelving unit on the wall that matched the desk she'd built for Saffron. She grabbed a broom and began sweeping up the floor.

Since they had arrived to start this project, she hadn't spent much time in Lurton. Each morning, she drove in to town, got started working, ate her packed lunch, finished for the day, then drove home. It would be decent to at least patronize a few establishments while she was in town.

Her back jean pocket vibrated. She pulled her

cell phone out and took in her brother's name on the screen.

"Hello, big brother," she answered.

She and Troy were as close as brother and sister could be. She'd kept him and her parents in the dark about her and Bobbie's tumultuous relationship. Shekita had at first thought she would be able to handle Bobbie, but it had soon spiraled out of control, and she'd found herself lying and hiding things from her family.

"Hey, sis. How is everything going?" he asked.

"Not bad. We are just finishing up for the day and will be heading out soon."

"What? You're not working late?" He chuckled.

"Nah, not today. They guys are wanting to go out for drinks here in Lurton and are dragging me with them. I didn't have the heart to tell them no." She lifted the oversized dustpan and walked out into the hall where a large trash can sat. She emptied the dustpan into it. She glanced toward the front and didn't see anyone. She smiled and headed back to the office.

"It would do you some good to get out. You work too hard."

"And because of my hard work, we should be

done with this project a few days early," she boasted. She was proud of the timeline they had kept to. She would admit she was a workaholic and had stayed late multiple times. The town ice cream shop was important. The children of Lurton needed to be able to come and get their frozen desserts.

"There are six respectable men on that project that will get the job done. You need not try to do it all on your own."

Her brother was always the voice of reason. He knew she was a hard worker and a perfectionist. When they were younger, it was he who'd helped start her on creating with wood and building things. She loved crafting beautiful pieces of furniture and giving them one-of-a-kind designs.

She put up the broom and dustpan and walked through the building, shutting off the lights. She made it to the front and found herself alone. She chuckled and grabbed her bag and hefted it up on her shoulder. Her phone vibrated, signaling a text. She glanced at it and found Mike had texted her the address to the bar.

"Was there anything in particular you wanted, dear brother?" she asked. Not that she minded him calling, but she was sure it was for a reason. Shekita did one last sweep through the shop then exited the building. She locked the door and headed toward her truck.

"Do I need a reason to check in on you? It's getting late, and I didn't want my sister working late five days a week." He laughed.

She scowled, because apparently, he knew her too well.

"And, Mom told me to call you to let you know that Sunday she's cooking and we are to be there."

Shekita's mouth watered thinking of what her mother could potentially be cooking up. Her food was famous. It was amazing that the entire family wasn't grossly overweight. Jolinda Harper's love language was food. She enjoyed feeding her family and ensuring they were well-fed at all times. It didn't matter the time of day, if Shekita called her mother hungry, there would be a hot plate waiting on her when she arrived at their home.

"Of course I'll be there." She laughed. Shekita arrived at her truck. She opened her door and tossed her bag in the back seat. She took a look at herself in the back-door window and grimaced. Going out drinking at a bar in a flannel shirt and jeans wasn't flattering. She never knew who she would meet. She unbuttoned her shirt and removed it. She threw it in the back to join her bag. A white cami and jeans would do. She glanced down at her feet and kicked off her steel-toed boots. She tossed them in the back to join her growing pile of items. She hopped in and snagged her flip-flops that were resting on the floor of the passenger seat and slid them on her feet.

Now, that was much better.

"Will you be bringing anyone?" he asked.

"Seriously? You are going to ask that?" She scoffed. She turned her vehicle on, and the phone flipped over to the Bluetooth connection of her vehicle. She popped her phone in the holder to free up her hands. Thankfully, she kept some items in her car to allow her to freshen up. After brushing her hair up in a ponytail, hitting her pits with a fresh layer of deodorant, a spray of her favorite perfume, and applying a fresh coat of lip gloss, she felt like a new woman.

"I don't mean anything by it. You don't talk much about your personal life after you know who," he said.

Shekita closed her eyes and exhaled. It was hard to talk to her family about her love life.

She had thought she had found the one she was going to spend the rest of her life with, but that was a massive fail. She'd been so wrong about Bobbie.

The woman she had thought she'd love had turned into a psychopath who would rather hurt her than love her. Shekita had suffered not only mental abuse but physical at the hands of Bobbie.

"No, there is no one," she grumbled. She threw her car into gear after inputting the bar's address in the GPS. The guys apparently hadn't wanted to wait on her. They'd better get a good table and save her a seat. "Got any friends who have single sisters?"

"I'll keep my ear out for you." Troy barked a laugh.

"You'd better, and tell Mom I'll be there. Alone." She groaned. According to the GPS, the bar wasn't far from the ice cream shop. By the looks of it, she would be arriving in two minutes.

"I will, and have fun tonight. Drink a lot and get hungover. It won't hurt if we miss one day on the ice cream shop. You all deserve it for your hard work."

They disconnected their call with the promise to talk tomorrow. Shekita turned the corner and saw the sign of the bar.

The Dirty Habit.

She smirked at the name. It had the appearance of a log cabin with a porch that wrapped around it.

The backdrop of the establishment was a gorgeous mountainous range off in the distance. There were rows of motorcycles parked out front, and the lot was almost full. She quickly found a spot then made her way to the entrance.

The bouncer at the door was tall and had muscles on top of muscles. She would be surprised if he wasn't a bear shifter or something of that nature. He gave her a nod and held the door open for her. She hefted her bag on her shoulder, offered him a smile, and went inside. The moment she crossed the threshold, she was assaulted with loud country music blaring from the speakers. The scent of cigarettes, weed, and good food was thick.

Shekita inhaled and smiled. The guys had been right. She needed to get out and relax. They had been working hard on the job and were owed a night out on the town. Troy was right. She deserved to go out, get drunk, and have one hell of a hangover.

That was what she was going to do. It had been a long time since she'd gone out and gone home with someone. She only hoped to be so lucky. Shekita scanned the establishment, taking in the throng of bikers, cowboys, and other patrons that filled the bar from wall to wall. Even the dance floor was packed with gyrating dancers moving to the rhythm of the music.

Her gaze landed on a bunch of raised hands trying to get her attention. She laughed at Hector who stood and sent a sharp whistle through the air.

How many drinks had they had without her?

She navigated her way through the bar and finally arrived at their table. They all shifted around it, giving her a newly opened seat.

"Boss lady is here!" Mike hollered. He instantly slid a shot glass filled with a clear liquid in front of her.

Warren grabbed a chair from somewhere and returned to the table. He took his seat and raised his glass to her.

"It's about time, boss," he joked. He motioned to the round of drinks on the table in front of them. "I made these knuckleheads wait for you to get here before we got started."

"That's so kind. You all didn't waste any time getting here," she grumbled. How fast had they driven, and when had they left the site?

She raised her glass, and they all followed suit. She glanced around the table and took in her team. Mike, Rudy, Hector, Warren, Ryan, and Tim were hardworking men who she could count on.

"Harper Construction. The best damn construction crew," she said.

"Harper Construction," they echoed.

She knocked back the shot of vodka and slammed her glass down on the table. It felt good to be out with the guys. This was just what she needed. The Dirty Habit was fast becoming a place she could see herself returning to.

Two rounds later, Shekita had a nice buzz and was feeling great. It looked as if she would be getting a hotel tonight. There would be no way she would be okay to drive. She wasn't fully drunk, but she planned to get there. Her brother was right. One night to just forget all responsibility was what she needed.

"Next round is on me," she shouted.

The guys cheered, raising their frosted beer mugs to her. Hector had disappeared some time ago. The last time she'd seen him, he was hugged up with some female out on the dance floor. The other members of the crew were chilling around the table, watching the sports show on the closest television.

After flagging the waitress down and placing their order, she stood and scanned the crowd. If Hector could find company, she could, too. There was no point in just sitting at the table. The music the DJ was playing was catchy. She tapped her foot to the rhythm of the beat. Her gaze landed on a familiar couple. Saffron and Dasha were sitting at the bar.

"I'll be back," she said, patting Warren on the shoulder. There was no time like the present to go chat with the women who had hired her company.

CHAPTER THREE

"Thanks again for coming with me," Pola shouted over the music. It had taken much persuasion to get Dasha to come with them. Saffron hadn't minded coming out with her. It was almost like the good old times except her brooding sister was in attendance. The moment she'd seen Saffron's dress, she'd put her clothes on and agreed to come with them.

Pola knew it was the bear in her sister.

Bears could be quite possessive of their mates. She wouldn't want anyone, male or female, sniffing around her mate. Even though Saffron carried Dasha's mark, it wasn't enough.

"I'll be your wing woman tonight." Saffron laughed.

She leaned against Pola while they stood at the bar. The Dirty Habit was packed tonight, and the atmosphere was electric. Pola and Saffron used to come a couple times a month to hang out. Their food was out of this world, and the drinks were top-notch. None of that watered-down stuff that some bars served, trying to cut back on expenses.

"Well, I'm glad Dasha drove. I don't have to worry about a ride. If I don't find someone to go home with tonight, then there will be lots of drinking and praying I get drunk." Pola snickered. It was hard for a shifter to get inebriated. Their metabolism burned through alcohol at record speeds, so it was actually quite rare to see a shifter shitfaced drunk. She may feel extremely nice, but fall-out-on-her-face drunk would be hard to achieve.

"Of course. We haven't got to celebrate the new job properly. Isn't that right, babe?" Saffron snagged Dasha's hand and brought her closer to her.

Pola could admit she was slightly jealous of the two. She wanted what they had.

Dasha erased any space that had been between

the two of them. Dasha wrapped her mate in her arms and pressed a kiss to the top of her head.

"We haven't. I'm proud of you, sis. The alpha and beta are lucky to have you running their office," Dasha said.

Pola's heart stuttered at her sister's sentiments. It meant a lot to her. Dasha was a woman of few words, and if she said she was proud of her, then she meant it.

"Thanks." Pola couldn't keep the grin off her face. She reached up and tucked her thick hair behind her ear. She waved down the bartender.

He jogged over to them and took their orders.

"I got this," Dasha said, whipping out her credit card. She slid it across the counter to pay for their drinks. "You are not paying tonight."

"I'm not going to argue with that." Pola laughed, holding up her hands. She inhaled, scenting a wonderful hint of a floral aroma. She frowned, not sure where it was coming from. The bar held the smells of cigarettes, food, and a fine undertone of sweat and body odors.

Saffron peeked around Pola and grinned. She moved around her toward someone. Pola turned around and found Saffron hugging a beautiful brown-skinned woman with dark hair. Pola was frozen in place as she watched her laugh and smile at Pola. She was dressed in jeans, flip-flops, and a white cami that highlighted her ample bosom.

Pola breathed in again, and the scent coming from her was familiar.

"Shekita, you remember my mate, Dasha." Saffron pulled the newcomer over with her.

The woman's smile was mesmerizing. She waved quickly at Dasha who jerked her head in a nod to her. The breath in Pola's chest escaped her. Her bear stood to attention, watching the brown-skinned goddess. She had a glow to her that spotlit her beauty. Pola wanted to get to know her.

Intimately.

"And this is my best friend, Pola Prime. Pola, this is Shekita Harper. She's the one who designed and made my office desk," Saffron said.

Pola extended her hand to the small woman. She inhaled her wonderful scent again, sending her bear into a frenzy. It was the same scent she had picked up on back in Saffron's office. It was alluring and dominated the air around her. Shekita slid her hand into Pola's, taking it in a light handshake.

"You do amazing work," Pola said, finally able to get her tongue unstuck from the roof of her mouth.

Shekita moved between Pola and Saffron, leaning against the bar.

"Thanks. I wanted to do something special for Saffron, and she gave me full creative reign to design her office. I'm working on her shelving units now. They should be done soon." Shekita's gaze dropped down to Pola's lips for a moment. She turned back to Saffron.

They fell into a conversation, speaking about the ice cream shop and the progress.

Pola's heart skipped a beat. Her bear was impatiently pacing back and forth inside her.

What is it? she asked her beast. Sweat beaded on Pola's forehead. She already had a sense of what her animal was going to say.

Mate, her animal replied.

Pola swallowed hard. The scent of Shekita was becoming overwhelming. Her gums burned from her fangs pressing against them, demanding to descend.

"Did you hear me?" Saffron asked.

Pola blinked, focusing on her friend. She barked a laugh and sipped her drink again.

"I said, me and Dasha are going to snag a table. I'm hungry and will be ordering food." Saffron patted her stomach.

Dasha dropped a kiss on Saffron's shoulder and took her by her hand and led her away.

Pola's attention was snagged by Shekita who remained at her side. The woman sidled closer to her due to a few rambunctious guys stealing Pola and Dasha's spot.

"I'm sorry." Shekita laughed.

They were now pressed against each other. The woman was much smaller than Pola's six-foot frame. The top of her head stopped below Pola's chin. Pola bit back a groan at the feeling of Shekita's soft breasts pushing against her side. She was hit with Shekita's scent even stronger. The urge to grab her by the hand and lead her out of the bar was growing.

"Don't worry about it. I actually don't mind." Pola found her arm boldly snaking around Shekita's waist to anchor her to her. Her sweet, flowery scent was enveloping Pola, drawing her to her. She dipped her head down, her lips stopping at the shell of Shekita's ear. "You smell wonderful."

"Ha! I'm glad you think so. I just got off work and tried my best to freshen up before I came." Shekita's lips tilted in a sexy grin.

Thank goodness for Pola's shifter hearing. Had she been human, she wouldn't have heard her.

"Do you live in Lurton?" Pola asked. The town was small, but it wasn't like Pola knew everyone. Someone like Shekita, she would have taken notice of her.

"No, I don't. I live in Black Fish."

The town she'd named wasn't too far of a drive from Lurton. It would explain why they had never run into each other. Pola's mind raced with the logistics of going back and forth from Lurton to Black Fish.

Slow down, girl. She inhaled. She would have to figure out if Shekita would be into her. Humans weren't like shifters, they didn't recognize their mates from their internal animals. For humans, it was different. Pola grew slightly frustrated at the notion that she couldn't follow her basic instincts and claim her mate. She would have to ensure that Shekita fell for her before adorning her with a claiming bite.

"Are you here by yourself?" Pola asked.

She tightened her grip on Shekita, taking notice that the woman wasn't pulling away from her. If anything, she leaned farther into Pola's embrace. For her to work in construction, Pola would have guessed she would be riddled with hard muscles, but there was a softness to her hips, stomach, and those full breasts of hers. Shekita may be a contractor, but she was definitely all woman. It was as if she were an oxymoron, and Pola was already in love with her body.

"Some of the guys from my crew are here, too. We needed to release some stress." Shekita tilted her head back. Her small, blunt white teeth snagged her plump bottom lip.

Pola stared at it, wishing it was her teeth nibbling on Shekita's lip.

Take her, her bear growled.

Stand down, Pola growled back. What did her bear want her to do? Lift Shekita onto the bar and claim her?

Her bear had the nerve to release a snort.

The music changed, and Shekita glanced over at the dance floor. Her body swayed to the beat of the song. It was a popular one by a country singer wailing about love being found in a field of daisies. Shekita's eyes fluttered shut for a moment, then they opened and focused on her.

"Please tell me you like to dance," Shekita said. Those teeth were on her bottom lip again.

Pola held back a growl, wanting to press her lips to Shekita's so she could run her tongue along them.

"I sure do." She snatched her drink from the counter and knocked it back. The cool burn of the alcohol slithered down her throat. She took Shekita by the hand and led her away toward the dance floor.

Shekita's body was pressed closed to hers. She gripped Pola's arm with both her hands as they maneuvered their way through the throng of people.

They found a spot in the thick of the patrons enjoying the music. Shekita's hands slid along her arms and came to entwine at the base of Pola's neck. They swayed together, their breasts brushing each other. Pola's hands found their way to Shekita's waist. They fit together perfectly.

Mate, Pola's bear snarled as if to remind her of what they both knew.

Shekita's lips were curved up into her sexy grin as she leaned her head back, presenting the column of her neck. Pola's fangs descended, bursting through her gums from her watching the object of her desire writhe in her arms. Shekita moved forward, closing the gap between them.

Pola leaned her forehead against her newfound mate's, gyrating her hips with Shekita's. Unable to resist, she covered Shekita's lips with hers. The kiss was explosive. Pola's tongue pushed inside Shekita's mouth, finding hers.

Everything around them disappeared.

Pola became lost in the woman in her arms.

Shekita pulled back slightly, but her arms were still entwined behind Pola's neck. Lust was heavy in her gaze. Pola picked up the strong aroma of her arousal. Her bear growled low, demanding they claim their mate immediately.

"I was going to ask if there is a woman in your life? A mate, maybe?" Shekita asked breathlessly.

Their bodies moved to the slow ballad flowing through the speakers. Pola took in the people wrapped up in each other's embraces, enjoying the song. Lovers kissing, hands roaming over bodies, it would seem they were caught up in their own worlds as well.

"I'm a bear shifter. We are not like humans and don't cheat. Once we mate, we are loyal for life," Pola whispered. She couldn't resist dropping a chaste kiss to Shekita's lips. She slid her hands down to the roundness of Shekita's ass, squeezing it gently. "When we find the one for us, they are our primary focus to bring that mate love, happiness, and pleasure."

"That sounds too good to be true." Shekita chuckled.

"But it is the truth," Pola admitted. She didn't want to stay in the bar any longer. She wanted to find them a quiet place, preferably her cabin, where she could take her mate. Already in the matter of a short time, Pola was finding herself becoming captivated by her. She wanted to take her far away from here, learn everything about her, who she was, what goals she had in life, what made her happy, and what made her scream in pleasure.

"It's hot in here. Want to go outside for some fresh air?"

Pola took in Shekita's hooded gaze, her plump lips, and knew she would follow this woman anywhere.

"Sure."

CHAPTER FOUR

Shekita's heart raced so fast it was hard for her to catch her breath. She didn't know if it was because she'd had a few drinks or if it was the sexy woman leading her outside.

They left via a side door that led them to the wraparound porch. The fresh air was cool and felt good on her warm skin. She breathed in the air, glad to be away from the thick smog of smoke. The nighttime sky was black, marred by the twinkles of the stars spread across it.

Shekita inched closer to Pola, holding her arm

against her chest while they walked along the wooden porch.

"It's beautiful out here," Shekita murmured. She glanced up at the bear shifter, and her core clenched with need. She had mentioned needing to release pent-up stress, and she couldn't think of a better way than with Pola. She didn't care that she had only just met the woman. One look in her eyes, and it felt as if she had known the bear shifter forever.

"It is," Pola replied. Her gaze wasn't on the sky but on Shekita.

They had arrived at the back of the building where the shadows covered them. Shekita moved to the railing and tilted her head back so she could watch the lights of a plane pass by. Her heart slowed with each breath she took.

"I'm talking about the sky." Shekita giggled.

Pola came to stand beside her, her warmth covering Shekita's back. The surrounding landscape behind the bar was a flat plain, sparsely covered with trees and brush. She could see clear through them to the mountainous range off in the distance. Essentially, they were alone for the moment, but anyone could walk back along the porch and find them.

"Then I guess we weren't talking about the same thing." Pola's head dropped to her shoulder. She dragged her fangs against Shekita's bare skin.

A shiver rippled through Shekita. She leaned her head away, presenting her neck to her.

What would it feel like to have those fangs bury themselves in her flesh?

It was unthinkable that she could have this type of reaction to another person. Shekita instantly felt a connection between her and Pola. She didn't know what it was, but she wanted to explore it. She felt safe in the center of Pola's embrace.

That she had never felt with Bobbie.

"You said before that you were looking to release some stress," Pola whispered. Her tongue skated along the column of Shekita's neck. Her arms tightened around Shekita's waist, bringing her flush against her front.

Shekita groaned, loving the feel of the woman's breasts pressing to her back.

"That I did." Shekita reached down and boldly grasped Pola's hand. She brought it up to rest on her aching breast. Her nipples were hard and growing sensitive. The soft cotton of her cami was an irritant.

Pola didn't hesitate in massaging her heavy

mound. Clearly wanting more, she took hold of the material and peeled it back, revealing her naked mound. Shekita hated wearing bras, and camis, with the built-in support, was a way for her to get around it.

The thrill of potentially being caught with Pola sent her heart racing. She was unaware of possessing a voyeur kink, but at the moment, she wouldn't be opposed to someone watching them.

"The scent of your arousal is calling to me." Pola growled. She pinched Shekita's nipple, tugging on it.

Shekita rested back on Pola, her eyes fluttering closed.

Pola's other hand skated along Shekita's belly. "I could help you with your desire."

Shekita's hands flew to the button of her jeans and undid it. She drew her zipper down as an invitation for Pola's hands. The bear shifter pulled her away from the edge of the porch and into the shadows. Pola reversed until her back was pressed against the building.

This was crazy, but Shekita was unable to resist. Her body was strung tight with the need for release. She parted her legs when Pola's hand slipped inside her jeans and underneath her panties.

Pola's confident fingers spread Shekita's labia and connected with her clitoris. She moaned, grinding against her finger. Pola pushed farther, dipping her fingers into Shekita's wetness.

"So fucking wet," Pola murmured.

She nipped at Shekita's neck, eliciting another moan from her. Her fingers returned to Shekita's swollen nub and rubbed soft circles on it. Her free hand continued to cup and fondle Shekita's breast, drawing the other side down and revealing her other one. Her hands trailed along it, giving it attention as she had its mate.

Shekita turned her head and reached up behind her to draw Pola's head down to hers. Their mouths connected in a deep kiss. Shekita's hips rocked against her hands, and she opened her mouth wider, allowing Pola's tongue to slide along hers.

Shekita felt wanton and abandoned all common sense that she shouldn't be out in the back of some bar allowing a woman to get her off. It felt natural. It was freeing, and she didn't want to stop. Her skin was on fire, and she wanted her clothes off her.

The kiss grew more frantic. Pola's fingers pressed harder on her sensitive bud. Her breaths turned into pants as she rode Pola's hand. Shekita's desires grew, the flames of her lust coursing through her body from Pola's hand on her breast. The firm grip on it sent an electric current straight to her core. She needed to feel those fingers inside her. Tears blurred her vision. She wouldn't be able to have everything she wanted at the moment.

"Yes," Shekita hissed, tearing her lips from Pola's. Her hips moved faster, trying to keep up the pace of Pola's nimble fingers. Desperation overtook her. The tendrils of her orgasm slowing rose inside her. It had been a long time since she had been pleasured to completion at the hand of someone else. She had taken it upon herself to bring herself to climax.

"Give it to me," Pola murmured. Her hand fell away from Shekita's breasts, exposing them to the cool night air. Her hand moved up, and she entwined her fingers in Shekita's dark hair and pulled her head back. "I want you, Shekita. Flood my hand with your release."

Shekita panted, her arms flailing around. She reached out and held on to Pola's arm. Her body was overtaken with tremors and spasms, and her orgasm slammed into her. Her cries echoed into the air while she rode the waves of her ecstasy.

As Pola had demanded, her release shot out of her, soaking her jeans and Pola's hand.

Shekita inhaled deeply. She had never climaxed that hard before. She fell back against Pola, spent. If it hadn't been for the bear shifter's arms, she would have fallen to the ground in a puddle.

"Spend the night with me," Pola whispered. Her soft lips brushed Shekita's neck. She withdrew her hand from Shekita's jeans and brought it to her mouth where she licked it clean. Her chest vibrated with a low growl. That sound shot straight to Shekita's core. "I need to drink your honey from the source."

Shekita's breath caught in her throat at the image of Pola's head buried between her legs. She spun around and pressed close to Pola. The shifter's head lowered, taking her mouth in a deep kiss with the promise of more. Pola ravished her mouth, her tongue filling Shekita's and dominating the kiss.

"Won't your sister and her mate miss you?" she asked, pulling back.

Pola nipped at her bottom lip with her fangs and shook her head. Her hands traveled up Shekita's torso and cupped her still-bare breasts. Shekita moaned, leaning into her hold.

"They won't and they would understand." Another kiss.

Shekita was finding herself barely able to keep

her hands and mouth off Pola. This time, it was Pola who pried her lips off Shekita's. "What about your crew?"

"They will understand. We are giving them tomorrow off. You remember, we needed to release some stress." Shekita grinned.

"The only problem is I didn't drive."

"I did."

Shekita tried to will her heart to slow down. She followed Pola's directions to her place. According to Pola, she didn't live far from the bar. She bit her lip, the memory of her orgasm replaying in her mind.

"Why did you cover these up?" Pola asked. Her hand snaked out and connected with Shekita's breasts. She rubbed on the hardened nipple that pressed against the cotton material.

"I didn't think it would be appropriate to walk past those people with my breasts hanging out." She giggled. She held back a groan, thinking of the men and a few women who were standing on the porch when they went to leave. She was sure they had all heard her crying out through her orgasm.

She'd eyed the ground, not wanting to hear their snickers or see the laughter in their eyes.

Pola, on the other hand, had strode past them with her head held high. Maybe it was the bear in her that was proud that she'd given Shekita one hell of an orgasm.

"Yeah, that wouldn't have been a good idea. I wouldn't want them seeing something that is mine." Pola snorted.

"Yours?" Shekita's eyebrows jerked up. She glanced over at Pola who shot her a cocky grin. The woman had the decency to shrug. They were speeding along a road in Shekita's pickup truck in the direction Pola had given her.

"Yeah. Tonight, you belong to me."

"Is that so?" Shekita gasped at the feeling of her cami being yanked down. The sound of it tearing filled the air. The white cotton material fell open, revealing her brown mounds.

Pola pulled Shekita's right arm away from the steering wheel. Her head lowered, putting her face in line with the exposed breast.

"What are you doing?" Shekita asked.

"Claiming what is mine." Pola's tongue snuck

out and teased her nipple. She pulled back, a twinkle in her eyes. "If I licked it, it's mine."

Shekita barked a laugh and took Pola by her hair and forced her to lift her head up.

"And you owe me a shirt." She motioned to her tattered cami.

Pola sat back and eyed her handiwork.

"I think you look better this way." She shrugged. She turned her attention back to the road and pointed. "Turn right there and then follow it all the way until you come to my place."

Shekita nodded. Pola had been right. Her place wasn't too far from the bar or town. Within minutes, she was parking her truck in front of a beautiful cabin. Shekita's mouth dropped open as she took in the large two-story home nestled in the thicket of woods. The front had oversized windows that would allow massive amounts of natural light in. The base of the home was stone walls.

"This is all yours?" she asked.

"I got a little carried away when I built the place. I wanted something that would be a forever home with my future mate."

Shekita felt the warmth of her gaze. She turned and looked at Pola. Her heart fluttered at the mention of *mate*. For some reason, thinking of Pola with someone else didn't settle well with her.

"It's beautiful. I can't wait to see it," she murmured.

"Come."

They exited the truck and walked toward the home. Before going up onto the porch, Pola leaned down in between the bushes by the stairs and dug in the ground. Shekita watched her pull a spare key from the dirt. Pola grinned and jogged up the stairs.

Shekita walked inside behind Pola. The contractor and woodworker inside her flared to life. The foyer was two floors, and the windows allowed the moonlight to shine brightly on them. Pola shut the door, and the slight echo of the lock engaging caused Shekita to spin around. Pola tossed the key onto the table near the door.

She advanced on Shekita, coming to stop in front of her. She reached out and cupped Shekita's cheeks in her hands.

"Do you want the tour now or in the morning?"

"Morning," she answered without hesitation.

Pola's growl sent a shiver through Shekita. Pola reached up and pulled the tattered remains of her cami off and dropped it onto the floor. Shekita had never buttoned her jeans back up, so it made it simple for Pola to push them down along with her panties. She kicked her flip-flops off and her clothing, leaving her naked.

Shekita inhaled slowly, watching Pola take in her naked form. She practically trembled while she waited. No one had ever looked at her the way Pola was. The woman was practically devouring her with her gaze. The fire in her eyes blazed bright, setting Shekita's body on fire. Desire flourished inside Shekita. Her pussy grew wet with the anticipation of what was to come. Somehow, she knew her life would change come morning.

"You are absolutely perfect."

Pola bent down and hefted Shekita over her shoulder. Shekita cried out, laughing. She tried to lift her head to catch any part of Pola's home, but she was unable to see due to her hair falling in her face. She wrapped her arms around Pola, hanging on for dear life.

She bit her lip, holding back a moan. She'd never been treated like an object of desire, only an object that was owned by someone. Bobbie had never showed a hint of desire the way Pola had.

Shekita felt sexy.

Desirable.

Pola climbed a set of stairs without an issue. She

was much stronger than she looked. It must have been the shifter strength that allowed her to carry Shekita. She was five foot four, a hundred sixty pounds. Not a light load, but Pola strode along without complaint.

Pola nudged open a door and walked into the room. She verbally commanded the lights to turn on, and to Shekita's surprise, they did.

"Oof." Shekita was dropped down on a very large, plush bed.

She pushed up on her elbows and met the heated gaze of her bear shifter. She bit her lip and watched Pola tug her shirt over her head. She quickly disrobed, standing before Shekita in nothing. She took in Pola's tall, six-foot frame. She was no small woman, her body was supple with firm, full breasts, a narrowed waist, hips that flared out, and a patch of thick hair that covered her sex. Her hair tumbled along her shoulders, her eyes glowing their amber shifter color.

Pola knelt on the bed and crawled toward Shekita who moved herself back to the middle of the bed. Her thighs fell apart, Pola bracing herself over her. A shaky breath escaped Shekita.

"Where are you going?" Pola asked. Her chest rumbled with another growl.

Shekita sensed that Pola's bear was near the surface. Her eyes revealed it, but hearing that rumble, it shot a wave a desire straight to Shekita's core. Pola rested a finger on Shekita's sternum just in between her breasts. "Tell me you are mine."

Shekita's gaze locked on the massive fangs that peeked out from underneath Pola's lips. Her breaths were coming faster as she pondered Pola's request.

You belong to her, a voice whispered at the back of her mind.

Somehow, saying those words brought an immense amount of pleasure to Shekita. Something was leading her to want to belong to Pola.

To want to feel her bite.

Shekita knew for a shifter to claim a human, they would have to leave their mark on them. Not that she'd ever been with a shifter before, but she had shifter friends and had learned of their ways.

"What are you saying?" Shekita reached up and cupped Pola's face. She pulled her bear down to lie on top of her. Pola's warm body felt amazing. She wrapped her arms around Pola's neck, unsure if she was reading the situation right. She didn't want to think of something as permanent as mating and claiming.

Fear still lived inside her when it came to

belonging to someone. She hated to admit that Bobbie had done one hell of a number on her. At one point in time she had thought she wanted to belong to Bobbie, but she saw how that had turned out.

Would Pola be the same?

Right now, she needed to feel the pleasures this woman could bring her. She didn't want to think. She only wanted to feel.

"You know what I'm talking about." Pola's eyes studied hers.

Shekita blew out a deep breath. She closed her eyes, and Pola rested her forehead on hers.

"Let's not talk about anything serious right now," Shekita whispered. She opened her eyes and met Pola's. The disappointment she saw was like taking a spear to the heart. "Let's enjoy tonight. Please."

Pola nodded, capturing her mouth in a mind-blowing kiss.

CHAPTER FIVE

Pola took her time exploring Shekita's body. Having her in her bed excited her. Who would have thought her mate had been living one town over this entire time. She was thankful Shekita's construction crew had needed a night out on the town. There was no telling if they would have met had she not come to the bar.

Pola pushed aside her disappointment that Shekita didn't want to talk about what was between them. It was more than a sexual attraction, but the slight hint of fear she scented from Shekita revealed that there was something Shekita was afraid of.

She also had to remember that Shekita was human. She may have some understandings of the way shifters were, but that didn't mean she truly comprehended.

Pola would have to be patient.

Her bear snorted at the thought.

Pola ignored her animal and continued licking and tasting every aspect of Shekita's body. When she arrived at her center, her mouth salivated at the aroma of her arousal. Pola's gaze settled on Shekita's pussy, and she inhaled, breathing more of her delicious scent in. A small thicket of dark curls nestled right above her hood, hiding her clitoris. Pola remembered the feel of the soft hair tickling her fingers back at the bar.

"Look at how pretty you are," Pola murmured.

Her fingers traced Shekita's labia that were slick and plump. She dipped between them for a moment, bringing her finger out. It was covered with a creamy white substance. She licked her finger, holding Shekita's gaze. Her mate's chest rose and fell as her breaths quickened. The taste of her exploded on Pola's tongue. She needed more of it.

Pola lowered her head and covered Shekita's sex with her mouth. Shekita's legs fell open all the way, resting on the bed. Her moan echoed through the air. Tasting her on her finger was nothing like lapping up her pussy and drinking it in for herself. Pola explored Shekita's cunt with her tongue.

"Pola," Shekita called out.

Her hand made its way to the back of Pola's head. She entwined her fingers in Pola's thick hair, holding her in place. Pola growled, lavishing her pussy with more attention. She paused and slid her tongue to Shekita's clitoris. She captured the swollen bud with her lips. She teased her by suckling and pulling on it. Shekita's hips rocked forward, and Pola applied more pressure.

She slipped one finger inside Shekita's slick channel. She was greeted by a tight sheath that contracted around her. Pola slid her free hand up to Shekita's breast, toying with her nipple. She was rewarded with a deep grunt rumbling from Shekita. Her hips demanded more from her mouth and her fingers.

In response, Pola eased another finger in. She twirled her fingers around, stretching Shekita's channel. She pressed them farther into Shekita, loving how she was not shy in taking her pleasure. More of her arousal poured out of her channel. Pola released her mate's clit and flicked it with her tongue. She wanted to ensure her lover would be fully pleased, so by morning, there would be no question who she belonged to. Her hand full of Shekita's breast, she focused on her nipple. She tugged on it, drawing a gasp from Shekita.

"Pola," Shekita called out again.

Pola thrust her fingers harder inside her mate, all the while continuously tweaking her nipple. She latched back on to her clit and sucked hard. She ignored the stinging in her scalp from Shekita holding on to her. Pola's arousal grew painful as she watched her writhe on the bed underneath her. "Yes, yes, yes—"

Her words were interrupted by a deep rising scream that flowed from her. Shekita's body grew taut, her hips lifting, then she was overtaken by her climax. Pola drove her fingers deep, Shekita's muscles contracting around her. Pola suckled her clit, and Shekita rode the waves of her orgasm. Her release flooded Pola's hand and the bed, but Pola couldn't care less. Pride filled her that she had extracted that type of response from her mate.

Shekita's body flopped back down on the mattress, but Pola wasn't done with her. She rose from the bed, withdrawing her fingers from Shekita's pussy. Her release had left Shekita very slick. Pola straddled her to settle her pussy on top of

Shekita's. She reached between them and positioned their clits on each other.

"I can't take any more," Shekita whimpered.

"Oh, but you can," Pola replied.

Shekita's eyes opened, and her lips curved up into a grin. Her hands came to settle on Pola's waist. Her gaze trailed down and locked on Pola's breasts. Pola rocked her hips, pressing down on Shekita. The mate of a bear shifter would have to have a healthy sexual appetite to match that of the bear. The fates would see to it. Shekita just hadn't tapped in to the potential of multiple orgasms through a single coupling. Pola was only too happy to show her how it could be between them.

"And you are just so sure I can take more?" Shekita chuckled. She reached up and brought Pola's chest to her.

Pola rested her hands on the mattress on each side of Shekita's head. Their hips moved in rhythm together. Pola watched Shekita lift her head and capture her nipple with her lips. Pola threw her head back, basking in the feeling of her suckling her breast.

"Yes," Pola hissed.

Their slick pussies writhed together. The pleasure was mounting inside Pola. She had waited her entire life for the moment where she would have the one person meant for her underneath her. She would do what she must to convince Shekita that they were meant to be together.

The scent of their sex filled the air, and it drove Pola wild. An ache spread through her that only her mate could satisfy. Shekita focused on Pola's breasts, switching to the other and bathing it with her tongue. Once she released it, Pola pushed her down to the bed and lowered her head. She captured Shekita's lips with hers, needing to consume all of her. Shekita's hands rested on her hip and the back of her neck.

Their slick cunts slid against each other effortlessly.

Pola released Shekita's lips and lifted herself. She grabbed hold of Shekita's leg and brought it to rest on her chest. She pressed kisses along it and continued to gyrate and rub herself on her mate's cunt. Her breath quickened as she her body grew flushed.

Shekita threw her head back, her hips meeting Pola with each thrust.

"Harder," Shekita cried out. One hand rested above her, grasping at the blanket, and the other settled on Pola's waist. She dug her nails into Pola's skin.

Pola ignored the pain and concentrated on the pleasure. She pressed a kiss to Shekita's knee and continued to ride her hard.

"Shekita," Pola growled. The rising of her release came for her. Her hips quickened; her hold on Shekita's leg grew tighter. Her sensitive nub caressed Shekita's, sending her on a spiral of ecstasy. Her basic instincts took over. She reached out and gripped Shekita's breast in one hand to anchor herself to her. She raised Shekita's leg higher, their pussies teasing each other.

Pola's control shattered. She cried out, slamming herself down on Shekita uncontrollably. Shekita's cry joined her as they reached their release together. Pleasure filled Pola's chest like she had never experienced before. She fell forward, landing on top of Shekita. Her mate's warm arms wrapped around her.

Pola buried her face in the crook of Shekita's neck and breathed in the scent of her. It would be too easy to sink her fangs in the meat of Shekita's shoulder and lay claim to her, but that wouldn't be right. Shekita had to willfully accept her bite.

She could feel the pounding of Shekita's heart.

It raced just as fast as Pola's. Shekita's arms tightened around her and just held her in place.

"I'm crushing you," Pola murmured.

"Don't move. I love the feeling of you on top of me," Shekita replied.

Their legs were still tangled together. Their bodies were slick with sweat and their release. Pola didn't care how much of a mess they had made of her bed. She loved the scent of sex and Shekita's arousal. If she could, she would cover her entire body in her aroma.

It was that addicting.

Her bear grumbled, upset she didn't claim Shekita, but Pola ignored her beast. Her animal was impatient and stubborn.

Pola shifted to her side. She was a tall woman and heavy. It wouldn't do her any good to finally find her mate then crush her to death. She rolled over and brought Shekita into her embrace. Her face was flushed, and she had the look of a woman who had been well loved. Pola reached up and pushed Shekita's wild hair away from her face.

"Are you okay?" she asked softly.

Shekita's eyes opened, and a lopsided grin appeared on her face.

"I don't think I've ever had three orgasms in

such a short matter of time." Her eyes fluttered shut. She snuggled deeper into Pola's embrace.

Pola relished the fact that she was seeking her out as her exhaustion overtook her. She smiled and rested her chin on top of Shekita's head.

Pola was awakened by a slight shift in the mattress. Shekita gently peeled herself off Pola and slid to the edge of the bed. She stood and padded toward the bathroom connected to Pola's master bedroom. Pola readjusted the pillow under her head and watched the door close.

Pola inhaled, taking in the scent of her lover in her bedroom. It belonged there. There were many times when she had been building her home that she had imagined the day she would bring her mate here. She wanted the house to be perfect for the other half of her soul. She had taken her time poring over the plans and layout. It had been her hope that when she finally brought that special person home, that person would fall in love with it as she had.

A grin spread across her lips at the memories from last night. She couldn't get enough of Shekita. Shekita's body was a wonderland that she'd got to experience. She had tasted every inch of her beautiful brown skin. From her plump lips to her dusky-brown nipples to her sweet sex that remained wet and ready for Pola. Shekita may not be a shifter, but her body certainly recognized Pola.

The sun was beaming through the glass windows. One thing Pola wanted when she'd had the house constructed was plenty of natural light and to still connect with nature from the inside. She rolled and sat on the edge of the bed facing the windows.

Now that it was morning, she needed to have the conversation that Shekita wanted to avoid. Pola tried to think of what she could potentially say to her. She hadn't thought she'd find a mate and one that was human. At that moment, she wished she could call her sister and ask her how she'd presented it to Saffron.

Pola bit her lip and fell deep in thought. She hadn't heard Shekita open the bathroom door until she was standing by the foot of the bed. Pola stood suddenly and spun around to face her. Her gaze fell to Shekita's naked form. Her mouth watered at the sight of Shekita. Her warm brown skin practically glowed in the sunlight. She walked over to Pola. She'd braided her hair while she had been in the bathroom. The style made her appear youthful and full of life.

"Good morning," Shekita said. She moved to stand in front of her.

Pola reached for her hand and entwined their fingers. She brought their conjoined hands to her lips and pressed a kiss to the back of Shekita's.

"Morning." Pola pulled her to her, closing the gap between them. The feeling of their bodies pressed against each other sent a rush of desire through her.

Shekita sighed and leaned into her embrace. Her lips tilted up into a soft smile. Her brown eyes studied Pola.

"Are you hungry?" Pola asked.

Her fridge had recently been restocked, and she had plenty of food in the house. What she wanted to do was cook a hot meal for her mate. It would show that she could provide for her. Her bear was wanting to take care of their mate. She was no Dasha when it came to cooking. Her sister had to be touched by angels. That girl could cook a leather boot and make it gourmet and delicious. Pola, on the other hand, did okay when it came to food. She'd kept herself alive all these years, surviving on more than what her mother cooked for family dinner night.

"What are you offering?" Shekita's crooked grin grew.

Pola's slid her hands down her back and rested them on Shekita's plump bottom.

"Well, I am a whiz at making boxed pancakes. I even think I've got some kind of breakfast meat and maybe some eggs." Now Pola wished she had paid attention to the food her mother had delivered. She sucked at grocery shopping so her mother had groceries delivered to her.

Shekita threw her head back with laughter. She reached up and cupped Pola's cheeks. Tears flowed down her face while she tried to stop laughing.

"Why don't you lend me something to wear and we can go check out your kitchen. I love cooking and can make us something."

Pola grinned and leaned down, pressing a kiss to Shekita's lips. Of course the fates would match her with the perfect woman. They would be two halves that fit together flawlessly. Pola wasn't the best cook, and apparently Shekita was.

"You sure you want clothes. I have an apron you can wear. That would be so—"

"Clothes, or at least a robe." Shekita giggled. She stepped back from Pola, breaking her hold. She rolled her eyes and rested her hands on her hips. Her gaze roamed Pola, heat flaring in her eyes. "You are much taller than me. Maybe I can just put my clothes from last night on."

"Oh, no. I have a robe you can wear." Pola raced over to her closet and grabbed two. She moved over to Shekita and handed her one. She sighed watching Shekita cover her perfect body. Pola put hers on, too, promising herself that their robes would be off soon enough.

Her stomach released a growl.

Yes, their robes would be off once they'd finished their breakfast.

"Come. Off to the kitchen we go." She took Shekita by the hand and led her out of the room. She wasn't going to miss out on a delicious home-made breakfast. She was a bear shifter, and good food was part of her love language.

CHAPTER SIX

Shekita sat back and placed her fork on the oversized island. She had been in love with the kitchen from the moment she'd entered it. The house itself was to die for. It was everything she would hope to have in a home. The craftsmanship was impeccable. This was a chef's dream. For a person who didn't really cook much, her cupboards were stocked to the brim. There was enough here to keep a family of five fed for at least half a year.

"What do you think?" Shekita asked, watching Pola shovel the food into her mouth.

"Um…" Pola paused and swallowed. She laughed, reaching for a napkin.

Shekita chuckled at Pola's embarrassed expression. She was actually pleased that Pola loved her cooking. She didn't need to hear her compliments. Her quietness while eating said it all.

Her cooking had never been appreciated before, so to see someone completely enamored by the food she had prepared brought a warmth to her heart.

"I don't know how you did it, but you are welcome to come here and cook anytime," Pola said. She took a sip of her coffee then offered Shekita a smile.

"Your kitchen is amazing, and you had everything one would need to make waffles from scratch."

"It must be my mother. She has groceries delivered and comes by once a month to stock my pantry."

"Your mother takes care of your pantry?" Shekita laughed.

A slow flush spread along Pola's neck and face. Shekita shook her head. She had been on her own since she was twenty, and her mother would never come and do anything like that. Shekita was very particular about certain things, and another woman putting her hands on any of her appliances would be an atrocity. Even Bobbie had never gone into the kitchen they'd once shared.

Shekita blew out a deep breath. She had to stop thinking about her. That was her past. She had broken free from her and now had a very promising future ahead of her.

Pola was the future.

Shekita ignored the voice at the back of her mind. She didn't know what was going on between her and Pola, but she wasn't ready to commit to anyone. Last night was supposed to be about fun and releasing pent-up tension.

"What is that expression for?" Pola asked. She stabbed her fork in the last of her waffles and swirled it along in her syrup, bringing it to her mouth. She chewed then swallowed. She motioned to Shekita. "You seem as if something is bothering you."

"It's nothing." Shekita shook her head. She didn't want to go into details about her previous relationship. She needed to put it behind her and leave it there in the past. Pola stared at her for a moment longer, reaching for her mug again. Shekita knew they had to discuss the elephant in the room.

Last night.

She stared down at her empty plate and wasn't sure how to bring it up. Did she just thank Pola for a fun-filled night, throw her clothes on, and leave? It had been a while since she had experienced a one-night stand.

"Okay, now what are you thinking? It appears you want to ask me something." Pola sighed. She reached out and rested her arm on the back of Shekita's chair. She dragged Shekita closer to her, putting their chairs directly beside each other. Her hand slid along Shekita's back in a soft, soothing caress. "You can ask me whatever you want."

Shekita was a chicken, she knew.

What was meant to be a one-night stand, she didn't know if she wanted it to be. She was torn. Get up and leave or stay and get to know Pola? Who said that after one night they had to commit to forever?

The look in Pola's eyes screamed she was trying to use the 'm' word. Shekita wasn't an expert on shifters, but she sensed that there was something deeper in Pola's eyes.

"Tell me about yourself. I know you are Saffron's sister-in-law, but I want to know who you really are." That was safe for Shekita. She had to admit she was interested in knowing more about the woman who had drawn more orgasms out of her than she'd ever had with any of her former lovers. Her body was sore in places she didn't realize had muscles. She lifted her gaze and met Pola's.

Pola leaned her forearm on the island and turned to Shekita. She appeared pleased that Shekita was taking an interest in learning about her.

"Well, I'm the youngest of three children. There's Dasha, our brother Junior, and then me. We are a close family. I grew up here in Lurton. I just started working for our alpha as her secretary. I love long nature walks and good food. I recently learned that I love pleasuring a certain brown-skinned woman who blew into my life last night."

Warmth flooded Shekita's face. Pola had gone above and beyond her duties in bringing pleasure to her. She had lost count of her orgasms after she'd had the fifth one. It was any wonder that either of them were able to walk this morning.

"Is that so?" Shekita asked. She squeezed her legs together to try to combat the ripple of desire that shot down to her core. She was naked underneath the robe, and it wouldn't take much for Pola to rip it off her. She swallowed hard—the vision of Pola doing just that sent her heart rate skyrocketing.

"Yes, and I want to know all there is about you, too," Pola whispered. She reached up and trailed a finger along Shekita's temple, her cheek, and her neck.

Shekita bit her lip and met Pola's heated gaze.

"Tell me, my sweet little Shekita. Who are you?"

Shekita swung around to face Pola. She eyed the woman who looked sincere in wanting to know about her. Shekita blew out a deep breath. She wasn't going to compare Pola with "she who will not be named." Pola appeared to be genuine and caring.

"Well, I grew up in Black Fish. There is just me and my brother, Troy, who owns Harper Construction. My parents are still alive and doing well. I grew up loving to work with wood and went into construction with my brother. He's been pushing for me to take more responsibility in the business and he promoted me to contractor. He can be so bossy, but I don't mind. The work is plenty, and the crew is a great one to work with. As you can tell, I love cooking, I love outdoors and working with my hands."

She didn't realize how close she and Pola were. She could see the few freckles that were scattered along her cheeks. She hadn't noticed them before.

Her gaze dropped down to Pola's lips which were plump and kissable.

"Why are you so nervous?" Pola asked.

"What?" Shekita jumped at her question. Nervous? Where did Pola get this notion from? She had tried to play it cool. All of this was new territory for her. She had imagined last night when she'd first arrived at the bar that she'd find someone she hit it off with, have sex with them, then leave in the morning before they had even awoken.

But that hadn't happened.

Instead, she'd found herself in the arms of a beautiful woman with bright-amber eyes, a mesmerizing smile, and had given her orgasm after orgasm.

"Why is your heart racing?" Pola's fingertip skimmed the column of Shekita's neck. Her legs nudged against Shekita's as she closed the gap between them. Her face nuzzled the crook of Shekita's shoulder. She trailed soft kisses along the soft span of skin that was exposed. "You do know my bear can sense emotions, and there is something causing your heart to beat fast."

Shekita found herself trapped in Pola's warm embrace. Her hand came up to rest on Pola's leg. She tilted her head away to present more of herself to Pola. Everything this woman did had her body on edge. She felt the sharp sweep of her fangs coasting along her skin. Her fingers moved, brushing the tie of Pola's robe.

"Well, it would appear you have an unfair advantage over me. I can't scent things, nor do I have an animal inside me that enhances me," Shekita murmured. She lifted her gaze and met Pola's heated one. "I'm just human."

"Am I supposed to shy away because you are not like me? I love the fact that you are human. I love that you sought out what you needed the most and I was able to provide it for you. What I don't understand is why you are holding back. I'm a bear shifter, and I will tell you that my bear wants you." Pola pressed a hard kiss to Shekita's lips.

She gasped, and Pola took advantage of it. Her tongue pushed forth, dominating Shekita's. Pola gripped Shekita's hair and forced her head back. She tore her lips from Shekita's and ran her tongue along the full length of Shekita's neck.

"I will give you all the time you need, and when you are ready, my mark will go here."

She bit Shekita gently. Not enough to break the skin but enough to get her point across. The slight pain sent a jolt of desire through Shekita. Her pussy flooded with her juices. A moan was ripped from her lips.

"Are you saying I'm your…?" Shekita swallowed hard.

"My mate," Pola growled.

Shekita whimpered from the sound of Pola's animal being so close to the surface. Was she ready to be in a relationship again? With shifters, a mating meant forever.

But Pola had just promised her time.

Shekita could admit she was afraid. She couldn't afford to fall into another relationship with someone who was like Bobbie. She wouldn't survive going through something like that again. This internal battle was weighing heavily on her. The past was the past. She had to move on and go toward the future.

Was Pola her future? There was one thing she knew already.

Pola wasn't Bobbie.

She'd known her for less than a day but sensed they were complete opposites. How did she know this? Deep down inside, Shekita knew she could trust Pola. The bear shifter wouldn't harm her. Her body ached to feel the passion that Pola had wrung from her.

She gripped Pola's robe ties and pulled, opening it. Shekita's breath caught in her throat at the sight of Pola's creamy tan skin being revealed. She stood and pushed Pola's robe off her shoulders.

"I need time," she whispered.

Pola stood from her chair with a growl. She reached out and snatched Shekita's robe from her. The material tore from Shekita as if it were thin paper. She tugged Shekita to her, closing the small gap between them. Their breasts grazed each other, sending another wave of desire through Shekita.

Pola lowered her head, pausing when their lips touched each other.

"Then time you shall have."

CHAPTER SEVEN

"So where did you disappear to the other night?" Saffron asked.

Her friend's eyebrows were raised high as she watched Pola. It was Sunday afternoon, and they were over at the Prime family home for their monthly dinner. Pola and Saffron were seated on the back porch. Dasha and their mother, Theola, were in the kitchen cooking dinner. The oversized rocking chairs were comfortable and perfect for gazing upon nature.

The Prime men had shifted and gone out in the woods hours ago. Pola was sure by the time her brother and father returned, their appetites would be ravenous. They would do their manly bonding things while out there. Pola would have loved to shift and stretch her bear's legs, but she didn't have the heart to leave Saffron alone. Theola and Dasha were not allowing anyone in the kitchen while they cooked. Too many people in Theola's domain made her mother one grouchy bear. Pola would probably talk her and Dasha into shifting after their meal.

Pola picked up her glass of lemonade and wasn't sure if she wanted to tell her best friend everything, but then again, Saffron knew everything there was about her. She couldn't keep a secret like this from her. Even though Saffron had held back a big one of her own.

Her relationship with Dasha had been unknown to everyone. When Pola had found out, she confessed she was a little hurt by their secret, but she'd got over it quickly. Pola recognized that Saffron and Dasha were made for each other. She couldn't have picked out better mates for them. The two were madly in love with each other.

"I'm sure you weren't even looking for me. You and Dasha haven't been able to take your eyes or hands off each other since you got together."

"Don't try to change the subject on me."

Saffron wagged a finger at her. She leaned on her armrest toward Pola. "Answer me. Where did you disappear to? And with whom?"

"All right, if you must know, I hooked up with someone," Pola admitted.

Saffron howled with laughter. She clapped and did a little dance in her chair. Pola couldn't help but laugh at her friend's antics.

"I want to know all the slutty details and who you burned up the sheets with." Saffron took a sip of her drink but didn't take her wide eyes off Pola. "And don't leave nothing out."

"Excuse me? There are some things we just can't share anymore now that you are mated to my sister." Pola laughed.

Saffron's mouth dropped open in shock.

"Are you still going to stick with that?" Saffron flopped back in her chair and pouted.

"I seriously don't want to know about your sexscapades with my sister." Pola shuddered. She loved her sister dearly but she didn't need to hear about the intimate details of their sex life. There were just some things she did not need to be briefed on.

"Well, fine, but just know that your sister is really good—"

"Ah… I don't want to hear." Pola covered her ears with her hands.

Saffron stuck her tongue out at her. Pola returned the gesture and laughed.

She was going to put Saffron out of her misery. "If you must know, I took Shekita home with me."

"Shekita, as in my contractor who is overseeing the renovation of my shop?" Saffron squealed.

"Yes, the one and the same." Pola sighed. Just thinking of her mate awoke her bear. If she closed her eyes, she could still taste Shekita on her tongue and hear her soft moans when Pola suckled her breasts.

Pola faced a challenge. There was something keeping Shekita from readily accepting the fact that Pola's bear identified her as Pola's mate. Pola didn't think it was ignorance of the shifter way of life. It was something else. There was fear in her eyes that was obvious to Pola. She didn't know who or what had put it there, but Pola was going to succeed at claiming her. She would ease any doubts and prove that she would be a good mate.

"What's wrong?" Saffron asked. Her hand settled on Pola's arm.

Her best friend could always sense when something was wrong. If Pola didn't know any better, she would assume Saffron was part empath.

Pola stared off into the yard that was surrounded by lush trees and greenery. The thick forest that backed their property was beautiful, but it didn't bring joy and happiness as it usually did.

"She's my mate." Just saying those words brought a sense of relief to Pola. She hadn't said them aloud before, and doing so gave her the determination to figure out how she could convince Shekita of the same thing.

"That's wonderful news, but why do you look so sad?"

Pola hesitated before answering. How did she explain to her human friend that she was disappointed Shekita didn't share in her excitement that fate had revealed they belonged together? All shifters put their trust and faith in the belief of fated mates. From the moment she had been born, it was already decided who would be the perfect person for her.

Shekita Harper.

Some shifters went their entire lives without ever finding their destined mate. Those who wanted companionship may take a mate of convenience.

They may even grow to care for their partner, but it would never be the love of a fated mate.

"Did she reject you?" Saffron asked softly.

Pola winced at her words. She didn't want to think what would have happened if Shekita had rejected her. Pola wouldn't be able to force a mating on her. That went against the laws of all shifters.

She hadn't said no. Which was a good thing. Pola didn't know how she would have reacted if Shekita had shunned her. Shekita had asked for time. Now that Pola had found her, she would give her all the time she needed. In the meanwhile, Pola needed to find a way to woo her mate. She needed to make sure Shekita understood that Pola would always care for her, love her, provide for her, and protect her.

"What did my sister do to convince you to mate with her?" Pola asked. She needed to pick Saffron's brain, and maybe her friend could help her win Shekita over.

"To be honest, I was interested in your sister. I know I didn't tell you this, but I went over to her house and took her some wine." Saffron sat back with a bashful look on her face. "So honestly, when we realized we were mates, it was easy to accept. It explained the attraction between us. Everything just felt so natural."

"That's beautiful," Lola said. She reached out and took Saffron's hand in hers. She gave it a big squeeze and offered up a smile.

"One thing I can say is you are going to have to get to know her. Get her to open up and talk. Maybe she's just getting out of a bad situation. If that is the case, then it will be hard for her to trust you."

Pola would have her work cut out for her. She would be willing to do what she must to win Shekita over. She would take her out so they could have a first date. This would allow them to get to know each other and spend time together that was not in the bed.

No naked wrestling in the bed until they truly knew each other. Pola bit back a sigh. This would be extremely hard. Her mate's body was a temptation, and the sweetness between her thighs would be a weakness she would have to sacrifice.

Her bear growled low. It would appear she didn't agree with the plan.

This has to be, Pola said. *We don't want to scare her off. Just have some patience.*

Her bear stopped her pacing and plopped

down. She would pout but she recognized the importance of possibly losing their mate.

We are going to woo our mate and win not only her trust but her heart.

"You and the guys have fun?" Troy asked.

Shekita shoved her fork in her mouth and chewed her food extremely slowly. It was Sunday, the day they were to have a family dinner. Her mother, Jolinda Harper, did not disappoint. She had made all of Shekita's favorite dishes. Smothered chicken with gravy, mashed potatoes, greens, cornbread, and a cream cheese pound cake for dessert.

Shekita was in heaven.

The only problem was they were sitting at the family dining table and all eyes were on her. She finished chewing and reached for her drink in an attempt to stall. There was no way she was telling the entire truth with her parents within earshot.

"Yeah, we had a lot of fun. I think a night out was what we all needed. You should have joined us." She took a long pull of her drink, setting the glass back down.

"You didn't go with them?" their father, James, asked. He wiped his mouth with a napkin, dropping it on the table. He raised an eyebrow at Troy. "If it was a reward, the owner of the company should have attended and paid for everything."

"I know, and I really would have loved to go, but I was at a dinner meeting myself." Troy's lips slid into a wide grin.

Shekita could already feel he had some news for them. Hopefully, this was the change in subject she needed. Troy wiped his mouth with his napkin and tossed her a wink.

"Is that so? For what? A new project?" Shekita asked.

It was like her brother to keep their company busy. He was making name for them, and more and more businesses were calling them to arrange consults.

"Don't leave us hanging, son. What is it?" their mother exclaimed.

Chuckles went around the table at her enthusiasm.

"I had the opportunity to meet with the alpha of the Brown Claw. Eddie has heard such good things about us, and she visited the shop we are currently remodeling. She's interested in us renovating their clan hall. It hasn't been updated since it was built. This is going to be a huge job." Troy sat back, pride showing on his face.

"Troy, that is amazing!" Shekita clapped. She was so proud of her brother. A job this big would mean that their entire crew would be needed, and there would be a nice-sized pay. She returned to her food as their parents bombarded him with questions.

Doing a job for the Brown Claw would definitely put their company on the map. Shekita sighed, thinking of her bear shifter. Shekita didn't know when Pola had become her bear, but it did have a nice ring to it.

She paused. Didn't Pola work for the alpha of her clan?

The bear shifter had been on her mind since she had left her place. Shekita had never had this feeling for someone before. Even with Bobbie, she'd never felt a sadness or longing in her heart when she wasn't around her.

What was this?

Shekita wanted to see Pola again. She had asked for time. She wanted to take it slow, but now that she wasn't with her, she wanted to be back with her. Was she going mad? She just couldn't make sense of what was going on with her. It was obvious Pola's bear was wanting her. She had even eluded to the word *mate*.

Could they be mates?

Mating between shifters was serious, and it was forever. There was no such thing as divorce amongst them. At least not that Shekita had ever heard.

"What's got your attention, dear?" Jolinda's warm hand rested on Shekita's, breaking her out of her thoughts. Her mother's curious eyes were on her.

"Oh, nothing." Shekita smiled.

"Are you sure?" Jolinda raised an eyebrow at her. It was apparent her mother didn't believe her. Jolinda Harper knew her children and was always able to sense when things were wrong. "You haven't had contact with Bobbie, have you?"

"What? God, no." Shekita shook her head. Thankfully, her parents didn't know how bad the relationship with Bobbie had progressed. She'd hid as much from them as she could. If they would have known, it would have broken their hearts.

"I saw her at the grocery store last week. She

asked about you," Jolinda said. She squeezed Shekita's hand slightly and offered her a smile. "She said she would love to catch up with you."

"I don't ever want to see her or speak with her again. Next time you see her, you ignore her," Shekita snapped, pulling her hand back.

"What?" Jolinda gasped.

Shekita pushed back from her chair abruptly. Her vision blurred with unshed tears. She rushed from the dining table and went into the kitchen. She escaped the house through the double patio doors. She walked over to the edge of the porch and leaned against the railing. She blinked, a warm trail of tears skating down her cheeks.

She would never give Bobbie a moment of her time again. She'd taken enough from Shekita.

How dare she speak to her mother? Shekita angrily wiped at her cheeks. The woman should not have approached Jolinda, but Shekita recognized the game she was trying to play. And she wasn't going to fall for it. Bobbie no longer had a hold on her.

The sliding of the door snagged her attention. She glanced over her shoulder, relieved when she saw it was Troy stepping out of the house. He shut the door and turned to her. Concern was evident in his eyes.

"They probably think I'm crazy." A dry chuckle escaped her. She turned back to gaze upon the backyard.

"No, not crazy. A little concerned." Her brother came to stand next to her.

She blew out a deep breath and rested her head on his shoulder. They watched the scenery in silence. She owed them all an explanation. She couldn't keep hiding what she'd been through from them. Once she got this off her chest, then she would no longer think of Bobbie.

Maybe then she could move on with her life. Thinking of Pola and exploring what was between them was what she wanted.

"I'm thinking there was more to your breakup with Bobbie," her brother murmured.

"You don't even know the half of it." She sniffed. Another trail of tears fell. She wiped her face with the back of her hand. She had never been one to cry, and she grew even angrier that Bobbie was wringing this type of response from her and she wasn't even present. "But it's all behind me now."

"Is it?" he asked.

He wrapped an arm around her shoulder. He

was so much bigger than her that her head barely topped the center of his chest. Troy had always been protective of her. He was so easy to talk to and he never judged. Her parents were the same. Maybe that was why she hadn't wanted to tell them about the decline in her relationship with Bobbie. She didn't want to see them disappointed.

"I am," she whispered. She wiped her face again and glanced up at him. She didn't want this to turn into a pity party. It was time to move on, and the big man upstairs had ensured she would. Meeting Pola was meant to be. She was beginning to believe that. "I met someone the other night when we went out."

"I knew it." Troy laughed. His dark eyes twinkled when he glanced down at her. He gave her a squeeze, turning around and leaning back on the railing. His face lit up with excitement. He looked just like their father. Tall, broad-shouldered, warm brown skin, perfect teeth, and he kept his hair cut close to his head. He was a woman magnet, and it was rare her brother was alone on the weekend. "So, tell me about her."

A smile found its way to her lips when the image of Pola came to her mind. Maybe what she needed was someone like Pola.

"We met at the bar. She's Saffron's best friend."

CHAPTER EIGHT

Pola's hands flew across her keyboard. The report the alpha needed was almost done. She was thriving at her new job and loved every minute of it, but today, her mind was on her mate. She eyed the clock on the wall of her very cozy office and groaned. She had another two hours before she got off work.

She had a plan.

She was going to woo her mate.

No one could resist a cute, cuddly bear who brought snacks and good things to eat.

Pola smiled. She may not be able to cook as well

as her sister and mother, but she knew of a local farmer's market where she could pick up some great home-cooked foods she was sure Shekita would love.

"Hey, Pola."

She looked up. Her alpha stood in the doorway. Her bear immediately bowed down, submitting to the stronger bear. Eddie walked into her office and set a folder down on it.

"Alpha, how are you?" Pola stood and lowered her gaze in a sign of respect.

"Oh, please sit. We don't need formalities in the office. Your family and mine are extremely close, Pola." Eddie shook her head, a small smile playing on her lips. She was a strong woman who everyone respected. She was tall, which was no surprise with her bear genes. She even towered over Pola's six-foot frame. Her thick brown hair was held back from her face in a single braid. She was dressed casual in jeans and a dark shirt. "I need you to set up a meeting with this company, myself, and Selen."

"And the subject matter?" Pola lifted the folder. She browsed through it and saw proposals for renovations for their clan center. She grew excited. Their building hadn't been renovated before and had been a central part of their community since the early twentieth century.

"We are renovating this building." Eddie strolled around Pola's office. She ran her hand along the wall and sighed. "It's about time. This building is due for updates. I don't know why we have waited so long."

Pola's gaze landed on the header of the paperwork and took in the name of the company.

Harper Construction.

Her heart stuttered. This was Shekita's company. She bit back a smile thinking how fate was pushing her mate toward her. She would have to work with Shekita, be that she was the alpha's secretary. She had to hold back her giddiness. She dropped the paperwork onto her desk and took her seat.

"I'll send out the meeting request right away. Did you have a certain day in mind or where you would want to meet?" she asked, reaching for a notepad.

"The owner, Troy Harper, and I, had dinner the other night and spoke a great deal. He wants to come do an assessment of the building so he can offer us an in-depth analysis." Eddie strode over to the door. She paused and spun around, walking backwards. "See if they can come either this week or next and just work it into my schedule and Selen's."

"Will do, Alpha." She gave a little wave as Eddie disappeared down the hall. Pola kicked her shoes off underneath her desk and got to work. It wouldn't take her long to compare Eddie's and Selen's schedules then offer something out. Once she had a few dates in mind, she placed a call to Harper Construction.

A sultry voice came on the line. Pola was slightly disappointed it wasn't Shekita's. Not that she would expect Shekita to be answering the company's phones. She was soon connected to Troy's secretary, and they hashed out dates. After the call, she sent out the dates to the alpha's and beta's calendars.

Pola sat back and wondered if Shekita would be coming with Troy to do the assessment. That would give her another opportunity to see her mate. She wanted to share the history of her clan and people with her. Shekita would need to know about her people if they were to be mated. Pola knew without a doubt she would be able to convince her they belonged together.

The rest of Pola's day flew by. Not that she didn't love her job, she did, but she had more pressing things on her mind. She gathered her purse and keys then flew out of her office. She locked the door and headed down the hall to check in with the alpha and beta just in case they needed anything before she left. Thankfully, neither of them were in their offices.

Most times they weren't. The two were true bears and didn't like being inside. Pola chuckled and spun around on her heels and ambled through their clan's building. It was like a community center for their people. It was always bustling with activity. There were plenty of classes held here for the public, traditional meetings of the clan, mating ceremonies, and a small library of ancient books that were cared for by the clan's historian. It would do the building good to get an upgrade.

Pola slid into her car and tossed her purse in the passenger seat. She blew out a deep breath and wondered if she should happen to stop by the Lick and Bite, would she see Shekita. Grinning, she started the engine and put the car in gear. It didn't take her long to get to Saffron's shop.

Pola parked down the street, unable to get a close spot. She wiped her damp hands on the skirt of her dress and made her way toward the shop. It was a beautiful afternoon, and her bear was pacing inside her. It had been a few days since she'd last shifted.

"Okay. As soon as I get home later, you'll get to come out." Pola chuckled. Her bear pushed against her stomach. She inhaled the wonderful fresh air. She was riding on a high today. She smiled and waved to another pedestrian. Her bear head butted her again. "I promise. When we get home, you'll get to come out. Just not right now in the center of town."

The humans wouldn't appreciate a large grizzly bear scampering down the main road. She giggled at the picture. It would be funny, but she'd hear it from the alpha. Lurton was a mix of human and shifters. For the most part, everyone got along well, but it would still be a sight to see a grizzly walking along.

Pola arrived at the Lick and Bite. She took in the sign above the door and smiled. Her friend had worked hard for this shop. Leaving corporate America to work for herself had been a dream come true for Saffron. Pola was happy for her best friend to return home and settle down.

Pola swung into the shop and was assaulted by the aroma of fresh paint and loud, blaring music. The bright colors on the walls were a definite change from the white walls that were present before the place had burned down. Pola scanned the shop and took in a few men working, but there was no sign of Shekita.

"Can I help you?" A tall man with backward baseball cap on walked toward her. Paint was splattered all over his clothes and matched the walls. He appeared to be pleasant, offering her a warm smile.

"Oh, um, I'm Pola. I'm friends with the owner, Saffron. I was just stopping by to see her," she lied. Thankfully, he was human and wouldn't be able to scent her lie. She eyed the room again and didn't see Shekita. She inhaled, testing to see if she could pick up her scent. It was there, but faint, as if she'd left hours ago. Pola's shoulders slumped. She'd missed her.

"She's in her office or at the back doors. A delivery just arrived." He motioned to the hall behind the counter.

"Thanks." She wasn't sure he'd heard her when he went back to his work. She headed toward the rear of the store in search of her friend. She might as well make good on her lie. It would look weird if she just turned around and left.

She picked up on male voices, but she followed her nose and found Saffron in her office.

"Need some help with that?" Pola asked.

"Oh, my goodness. You scared the shit out of me," Saffron swung around with wide eyes. She was stretching high, trying to hang a picture on her wall. She barked a laugh and waved Pola over. "One of these days, I'm going to put bells on you and your sister."

Pola grinned and dropped her purse on a cushiony chair sitting by the door. The office was coming to life. Saffron was putting her mark on her domain. The office was homey yet functional with a splash of vivid colors. From a bright, hot-pink focus wall to softer variations spread throughout the office. With the bold furniture Shekita had crafted and softer feminine colors, it was perfect for Saffron.

"Well, we just need you to fix your hearing." Pola snickered. She lifted the picture and leaned her head against the wall to find where the hook should deposit. "You know it would be easier if you had a fork. It will help drastically."

"A fork?"

"Yes, a fork. Don't look at me like that," Pola said. She could feel her friend's gaze on her. "I saw it online. Using a fork will help. Google it." She finally found where the backing of the painting was.

It slid on the hook. She stepped back and tried to straighten it. "How's that?"

"A smidge to the left." Saffron moved back farther and eyed her handiwork. "A little more. There!" Her friend broke out in a wide smile.

"Wow, the shop is looking amazing." Pola turned around and walked over to the chair where her purse was. She picked it up and took a seat.

"Isn't it. The truck just arrived with the furniture for the dining area." Saffron hopped up on her desk and eyed Pola suspiciously. "Not that I'm happy to see you, but what's up?"

"Can't a girl just stop by and see her bestie?" Pola tried to look innocent, but from the doubt on Saffron's face, she was failing.

Miserably.

"Sure, but I'm going to go out on a limb and say it was a certain contractor you were looking for. I'm just the second choice."

"What?" Pola gasped dramatically. "You would never be second choice for me."

She batted her eyelashes and clutched her purse to her chest. She was putting on an Oscar-award-winning performance. How dare her friend not think she was coming to see her.

"Pola."

"Okay, yes, I was coming to see her." Pola slumped back. She felt like a stalker who had lost their target. She eyed her friend. "Am I that obvious?"

"Very, but I'm sad to report that Shekita left hours ago." Saffron's face softened. A small smile slid onto her lips. "Would it help if I told you she said she was heading home early."

Pola sat up abruptly. She grinned and flew across the room. She swept Saffron up in a hug, setting her laughing friend down. Of course her friend would help her.

"Thanks. Gotta go."

Pola's bear was on a mission. Once Pola had arrived home, she had to keep her promise to her bear. The plan had been to go for a quick run, return home to shower, then hop in her car and head to Shekita's. She had stopped by the farmer's market after leaving Saffron's shop. She had picked up two meals, a bottle of wine, and a dessert.

Everything she would need to woo her mate on a first date.

But instead of a quick run in her bear form, her bear had other plans for them. They traveled long and far.

Where are we going? Pola asked.

Mate.

Wait, what? Pola gasped. She couldn't believe her beast. *You turn around this instant. We were going to Shekita's house when we returned. I have presents for her back at home.*

Her animal didn't reply. The bear took off at a full run. The animals of the forest scurried away. The only sound around was that of her large animal trampling through the woods. Pola tried to take back over, but her animal had the nerve to push her back.

Mate.

Pola groaned. Her plan to go and woo her mate was apparently overturned by her stubborn grizzly. They had been traveling for over an hour. The sun was low. Nightfall would be approaching soon. Her animal was making good time, setting a steady pace.

You know this would have been much faster if I just drove. In the car, she snapped.

Again, her animal ignored her. Pola settled back and watched her bear navigate the region. She wasn't sure how her bear knew the exact area her mate stayed in, but shockingly, she was headed in the right direction of Black Fish.

Her animal skidded to a halt. A low warning growl vibrated from her chest. Pola sat up and took in the scent of another predator close by.

Another bear.

She couldn't tell if it was a shifter or a pure-bred bear.

Montana was home to grizzlies. There were at least a few attacks reported each year by the National Parks Services. Pola inhaled again. It was definitely a bear. Her beast went into defensive mode.

She eyed the property around her, taking in the thick brush surrounding her. Tall trees stretched toward the sky with their thick branches providing shade with their leaves. The area was beautiful, untouched by man. The woods were still silent, and it wasn't just because of her. Another predator was out there. She spun around and took in the scent behind her.

That was a plus. The bear was not in the direction they needed to go. She could try to outrun them, in hopes of avoiding a confrontation.

Her bear growled again, the hairs on the back of her neck rising. Her long talons dug into the soft dirt underneath her. The muscles in her body grew taut as she scanned the area, waiting for the bear to arrive.

No, we are not fighting anyone today. Remember? We need to go to our mate.

Her bear snapped out of it and moved in the opposite direction of the scent. It wasn't that often that shifters fought their natural counterparts.

Her paws pounded the ground, eating up the distance. Hopefully, the other bear wouldn't follow. It was probably by chance that they'd come near each other. Pola pushed thoughts of the bear to the back of her mind. After a full hour of running, her bear finally settled down to a slow walk. She was out of breath, but they had arrived at the outskirts of Black Fish. Her bear continued with no need for directions. It was like she knew exactly where Shekita lived. She settled back and let her animal guide them to their mate.

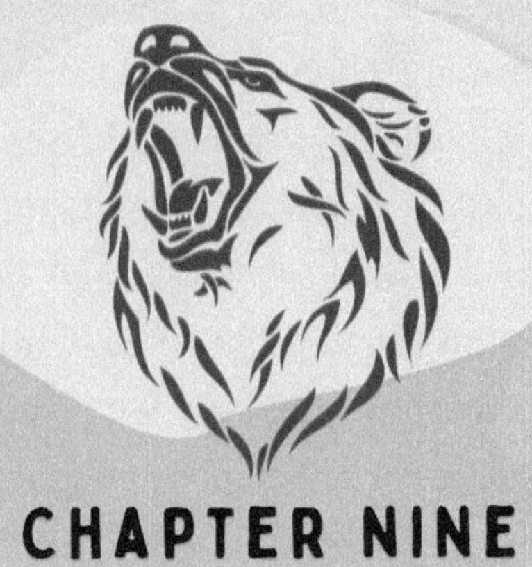# CHAPTER NINE

Shekita blew out a shaky breath. She stared down at her cell phone and the message on the screen. After she had left Bobbie, she had gotten a new telephone number. She'd wanted to cut off all ties between them. She'd requested a private one and only gave it out to those she felt needed to contact her.

So why was she staring at a text from Bobbie?

Two words.

Call me.

Nothing else, but Shekita recognized the telephone number. Who would give it to Bobbie? She closed her eyes and inhaled slowly, then blew out the breath. Her breathing exercises were something she had learned to calm down her anxiety.

She placed her phone on the kitchen island and stared at it. Thankfully, her mother hadn't given out Shekita's contact details. Her family had been shocked and appalled when she had finally come clean about the relationship. It had been hard to share something so personal with them but, as always, they'd listened. She had thought they would be disappointed in her, but they were quite the opposite. They had shown her unconditional love, and it was her who then needed to apologize to them for not telling them what she'd been going through.

They all made her promise to never hold anything in like that again.

"There was no reason for you to go through hell without us," her mother had whispered, tears flowing down her face.

"We would've helped you. One word was all you would have had to say, and we would have been there." Her father had wrapped her up in his arms.

The moment his voice shook, the dam of tears broke for Shekita.

She'd never seen her father cry before.

That night had turned into a one of healing and love for her.

But now, here she was alone, staring at her phone. She pushed away from the island and moved to the door that led to her backyard. She would not be responding. She was going ignore the message and push Bobbie out of her mind. The air in the kitchen was becoming stifling, and she needed fresh air. Exiting through the door, she walked out onto her stone patio, sat in her oversized chair, and rested her feet on the matching ottoman.

Evening had fallen, and the cool air was refreshing. She inhaled and immediately felt her body relax. Her backyard was her oasis. She had all the comforts of home outside. There were matching outdoor couches along with a fire pit in the center. There had been plenty of nights where family and friends had spent time around a roaring fire. She had hung strings of lights around the yard to provide light after dark.

Shekita loved to entertain and wanted to get back to it. Maybe she could invite over a certain bear shifter for dinner. She could cook a wonderful meal for them, and then they could come outside and light a fire in the pit. She had a big blanket they could snuggle under, watching the flames and the stars in the inky sky.

Shekita's heart warmed at the thought. A smile

formed on her lips. Planning a date for them would be fun. She had wanted more time, and dating would be the best way they could get to know each other. If they were truly meant to be together, then Pola wouldn't have a problem with doing things her way.

Satisfied with her idea, she planned a grand meal for them. She wanted to impress Pola. She didn't want Pola to only want her because of fate. She wanted Pola to like her for who she was.

With ideas brewing, she realized she was going to have to stop at the market. Excited, Shekita stood and stretched. She needed to go through her pantry, make a list, then run to the store first thing in the morning. She turned to walk back in her house but paused.

A rustling in the trees behind her yard caught her attention.

What was that?

The wind wasn't blowing that hard. She stared off in the direction of the sound. It was probably her overactive imagination. There usually wasn't much that would be in her little wooded area except rabbits, raccoons, deer, and the occasional possum.

"I'm losing it," she murmured. Her gaze wandered around her property, and she didn't see anything out of the ordinary. She eyed the woods again and froze in place.

A set of amber eyes met her gaze.

Whatever it was must be a large animal. From the height placement of the eyes, she knew she wasn't dealing with a small, docile creature.

A low growl sounded.

Definitely not a deer.

Shekita took a step backward. It would take her a few seconds to reach the door. Whatever it was would not be eating her.

A large brown grizzly bear emerged from the trees.

"Oh, hell no!" She cried out. She tried to get her feet to move but she was frozen in place, fear consuming her.

The bear slowly ambled halfway to her before stopping. It lifted its head, sniffing the air.

For some strange reason, there was an air of familiarity to the beast. Shekita relaxed slightly and took the time to study it. She couldn't make out much detail since nighttime had fallen. The lights around the yard only allowed her to see a little.

The bear returned her stare, not moving. If this was a crazed animal on the attack, it would have charged at her.

"Pola?" she whispered.

The bear's ears twitched in recognition. Shekita took a step toward the bear. This might be one of the most insane things she had ever done. If she was wrong, then she may pay dearly for the mistake. The bear whimpered as she drew closer.

"This is crazy."

She stopped in front of the bear and shivered at the sheer size of it. Power radiated from the massive beast. Its eyes were kind, and the longer she stared into the amber orbs, the more she knew she had been correct.

"Pola, your bear is beautiful."

The bear lowered her head and butted Shekita in the chest. She must want Shekita to touch her. Shekita reached out hesitantly, her fingers making soft contact with the dense fur. She was in awe of the softness as her hand traveled along her head.

Pola raised her head, sending Pola's heart rate skyrocketing. Their eyes met, and Shekita was sure this was Pola. The bear pressed her nose to Shekita's neck to nuzzle her. Laughter spilled from Shekita at the bear's antics. Her large snout was warm and tickled Shekita's neck.

"Let me speak with Pola." Shekita pushed on the bear's head and stepped back.

The bear hesitated for a moment. She rolled her eyes and whined.

"Please?"

After a hefty sigh, the air around the bear shimmered. Shekita was fascinated with the process. She had never been so close to a shifter transforming. The brown fur receded into warm tan skin. The massive body decreased in size. What was once a sizable and bulky frame, was now morphing into a tall, full-figured woman who knelt on the ground. Her thick brown hair fell forward, hiding her identify.

But Shekita already knew who was before her. The woman lifted her head, her hair moving aside to reveal her face.

Shekita had been correct.

The woman was Pola in the flesh.

And she was naked.

"Hey." Shekita gave a small wave. She was trying to hold Pola's gaze and was failing miserably. Pola's body was beautiful. She should never cover it up. Shekita swallowed hard and allowed her gaze to greedily roam Pola's body.

"Hey, yourself." Pola pushed off the ground and stood to her full height. She studied Shekita, folding her trembling hands together in front of her. She bit her lip and just stared at Shekita. "I hope you don't mind me just showing up unannounced. My bear was determined to come and meet you."

Shekita held back a sigh. It was cute how nervous Pola appeared. Shekita couldn't remember the last time a potential suitor cared enough about seeing her. She softened on the inside even more. The walls she had constructed were slowing crumbling.

"That's okay. She is beautiful." Shekita had never been that close to a bear. Not a shifter and not a wild bear. Her fingers twitched remembering the soft bristles of fur on Pola's head.

"I could scent your fear," Pola murmured. There was an air of concern appearing on her face.

Shekita felt the need to lighten the mood up. The situation could have been worse had the bear not been Pola.

"Well, of course. I wasn't expecting a bear to come from out of my woods. I was taken aback," Shekita sputtered. She barked a laugh.

Pola relaxed slightly. "Again, she really wanted to meet you," she said. She shook her head, her eyes narrowing on Shekita. "Why didn't you run? Not that I would recommend it, but most people's first instinct is to run from danger."

Shekita shrugged and moved closer to Pola. She took her hand and entwined their fingers. Something pushed her toward the shifter. She smiled at her, experiencing a flutter of butterflies in her stomach. Pola's hand tightened on hers.

"I just knew you wouldn't hurt me. I had a feeling it was you, and what's funny is, I was just thinking of you," Shekita admitted. Again, she was having a hard time keeping her eyes off Pola's tantalizing body. She swallowed hard and motioned to her home. "Want to come in?"

Now that Pola was here, she might as well stay. Pola searched her eyes, tilting her head in a slight nod.

"Of course. I'd love to."

Pola sighed. Shekita busied herself around the kitchen. Once they had entered her home, her little human had offered her a thin cotton robe to wear. It was cute how her mate's eyes kept drifting down her naked frame. The scent of her arousal had become overwhelming. Maybe it was best she was dressed. She didn't know how she would be able to resist her mate's delicious honey scent.

"Well, since you don't cook much, you are in good hands tonight." Shekita grabbed her oven mitts and slid them on to her hands.

Pola was enjoying herself watching her mate prepare a meal from them. The aroma of the food cooking had Pola's mouth watering. Her bear paced inside her chest, grouchy because they hadn't eaten in a while.

"There was never any doubt in my mind."

Shekita glanced over her shoulder for a moment then turned back to the oven. Something had passed in her eyes that Pola couldn't make out. It was a few minutes later, and Shekita was setting a plate down in front of her. Pola inhaled and bit back a groan. Her stomach rumbled from hunger.

"This looks amazing," Pola said.

Shekita grinned, carrying her own plate and took the seat next to her.

"I'm glad you think so. I wasn't expecting company tonight, but this will do," Shekita teased. She gently pushed Pola with her elbow. She stabbed her fork in the food and sent a wink Pola's way.

"Maybe someday this week, I can cook a real meal for you."

"This is much better than anything I would have been able to fix myself," Pola scoffed. She liked seeing Shekita so relaxed and in a playful mood. Pola dug into her food with much gusto. The flavors burst forth on her tongue. She groaned and continued shoveling the food in her mouth. The bear in her allowed her to eat large quantities. Now, her bear was famished. Pola eyed the stove and hoped there was more. She would be going back for seconds.

"Someone likes it." Shekita chuckled.

Pola paused and glanced over at her. Shekita was staring at her with a twinkle in her eye.

"I'm sorry." Pola reached for her napkin and wiped her mouth.

"No, don't apologize. If you're hungry, you're hungry. There's more for seconds." Shekita jerked her chin toward the stove.

They returned to their meal, eating in a comfortable silence. Pola's ears picked up the sound of a vehicle approaching. Her bear sat up with a low growl. Pola paused and wondered why her animal would be standing to attention. She set her fork down and reached for her drink. Taking a sip, she eyed Shekita who hadn't heard the vehicle. Pola had briefly forgotten that humans didn't have the sensitive hearing that shifters did.

The doorbell rang, breaking the silence.

"Who can that be?" Shekita set her fork down and hopped down from her chair. She took a quick sip of her drink and waved to Pola. "Stay here. I'll be right back."

She jogged out of the kitchen and disappeared from sight.

But for some reason, Pola's bear sensed something off. Pola unashamedly listened for Shekita as she opened the front door.

"What are you doing here?" Shekita said.

Pola didn't like the defensive tone in her voice. Nor did she like the slight hint of fear that resonated in it. Pola stood from the island and casually made her way out of the kitchen.

Whoever was on the other side of the door, their voice was muffled. Pola secured the ties of the robe tight. She strolled through the living room toward the front door and didn't see her mate. Shekita must have stepped out on the porch to greet the newcomer.

"Don't touch me," Shekita snapped.

Pola picked up her pace and arrived at the door.

The porch lights were casting the women in a soft glow. Pola peeked through the screen door. Shekita stood on the porch with a woman a few inches shorter than Pola's six-foot frame. The woman's head was shaved on both sides. Her long blonde hair was pulled up into a bun on top of her head. Her t-shirt was sleeveless, showcasing her full-sleeved tattoos on her arms.

But it wasn't her tattoos that captured Pola's attention.

It was her hand gripping Shekita's arm.

"Is there a problem?" Pola asked. She pushed open the door and stepped outside.

The woman's eyes flew to Pola. She scowled, turning her attention back to Shekita.

"Who the hell is that?" she snapped.

"It's none of your business," Shekita whimpered. She tried to snatch her arm away, but the woman held on. "Bobbie, you're hurting me."

Pola's bear slammed against her chest with a ferocious growl. Pola's gums burned and stretched as her fangs descended. She folded her arms in front of her and fought to keep control of her bear.

"Release her," Pola snarled.

"What? Am I supposed to be afraid of you?"

Bobbie gave a dry chuckle. She pulled Shekita to her, getting in her face. "You fuck her?"

Pola flew across the porch and gave the woman a shove, allowing Shekita to stagger backwards. She guided Shekita behind her. Pola stood to her full height, allowing her animal's growl to rumble from her chest. Her muscles were tight, and her bear was ready to push forward. But she couldn't allow her out. This Bobbie wouldn't stand a chance against a pissed-off grizzly bear. This fight, if it came to it, would be in her human form. It had been a while since she'd tussled as a human, but she would do it to protect Shekita.

"It might be best for you to leave," Pola warned. It calmed her bear to feel Shekita stand close at her back. Her mate gripped the back of the robe and remained where she stood. Pola narrowed her gaze on Bobbie. She didn't like her for many reasons.

For touching her mate and instilling fear in her.

"What are you? One of those shifters?" Bobbie snapped. She eyed Pola with hatred burning in her eyes.

Pola had to give it to her, Bobbie wasn't afraid of her.

She should be.

Her bear was pissed off and ready to do what she needed to protect her mate.

"Bear," Pola answered proudly.

It was then doubt appeared in Bobbie's eyes. She looked away briefly, a smirk on her lips.

"Well, isn't that dandy, but it doesn't have anything to do with why I'm here. So why don't you move out the way so I can talk with my woman—"

"Ex. We aren't together anymore, Bobbie," Shekita shouted from behind Pola. Her grip on the robe tightened. "I don't want anything to do with you, and there is nothing we need to discuss."

"You're going to talk to me, dammit," Bobbie roared.

She rushed forward to try to get around Pola, but she wasn't as fast as Pola's reflexes. Pola shot her arm out and pushed her back again. This time, the force of her strength sent Bobbie stumbling down the few stairs of the porch.

"This isn't over!" Bobbie rolled to her knees and slowly stood. Her chest rose and fell swiftly. She brushed her jeans off with her hands, spitting out curses. She glanced back up at Pola and Shekita who had moved slightly to Pola's side. "You're not going to have your fucking bodyguard around at all times, Shekita."

"Just leave me be," Shekita cried out.

"Go," Pola growled.

Bobbie had taken a step forward, then must have thought better of it. She whirled around on her heel and headed to her car. She yanked the door open, glared at them one last time, then got in, slamming the door shut.

The engine flared to life. The wheels screeched as Bobbie backed out of the driveway. Once she was in the street, she took off down the road. The red taillights grew smaller, then soon disappeared off into the night.

"We need to talk," Pola growled.

CHAPTER TEN

Shekita's body trembled uncontrollably. She followed Pola into the house and shut the door behind her. If this had not been a serious confrontation, she would have laughed at the fact that Pola had been ready to fight Bobbie in nothing but Shekita's too-small bathrobe.

Shekita felt Pola's heated stare on her. She hadn't turned away from the door yet. She didn't want to see what was in Pola's eyes. She also couldn't believe that Bobbie had found her new house.

Shekita had done everything she could to keep

Bobbie from knowing where she lived and her contact information. The only other thing she could have done was leave Black Fish. But then her family would have been distraught if she had moved far away. It would have meant getting a new job and all the things she didn't want to do.

It was unfair that it would be she who would have to start over just to get away from someone who had terrorized her at the end of their relationship.

"Is she the reason you don't want to talk about the elephant that's been sitting in the room?" Pola's voice was low and emotionless.

Shekita squeezed her eyes tight, bracing her hands against the door. She needed some type of strength to get through this conversation. Her knees grew weak and shaky. Slowly, she turned and leaned back against the door. Pola's face was void of any expression.

"She's part of the reason," Shekita whispered. She wasn't going to stand there and lie to Pola. There was so much that had happened between her and Bobbie that she had promised herself she wouldn't dive into another relationship until she was sure the person really cared for her.

Pola's bear chose you, a voice whispered in her ear.

Shekita's heart sped up at that notion. She had made herself a promise that she would only choose someone who would put her first, respect her, care for her, protect her. Someone who would never harm her but make her smile and laugh.

She met Pola's gaze and knew that person was standing in front of her.

She had been a fool.

Pola would be all those things if she'd let her.

"Is she who you would prefer?" Pola crept closer. She barely blinked waiting for Shekita's answer. She stopped where there was only a hair's breadth of space between them. Shekita tilted her head back, resting it on the door, so she could continue to meet Pola's gaze.

"No." Shekita's body trembled. This time it wasn't from fear but from desire. Whenever Pola was near, her body flared to life. She drew in a shaky breath and took in the scent of Pola. She smelled of the fresh outdoors. If she closed her eyes, she could imagine warm, cozy nights, a slight breeze, and the fresh scent of a storm brewing in the air.

It was funny she would think of a storm.

That was how Pola had come into her life.

The woman was a like a strong gust of wind,

knocking down all of her walls and breathing new life into her.

Pola rested her hands on the door, trapping her. Shekita didn't feel threatened by her at all. Pola would never harm her. It was something that didn't have to be said between them. She knew deep down in her heart that she couldn't avoid the inevitable.

She was Pola's mate.

And she should not deny what Pola knew and what she felt. Even though she was human, she sensed they belonged together. No one had made her feel how Pola did.

"Is this scent of desire that I smell on you for her?" Pola practically growled. Her fangs peeked from underneath her lips.

Shekita zeroed in on them. Her breath froze in her chest as she thought of those fangs piercing her soft flesh. To be claimed by a shifter, she would have to bear their mark. Her core clenched at the thought of being branded by Pola. Being cherished by Pola.

Being loved by Pola.

Shekita blinked, her breaths coming in pants.

She wanted Pola to claim her.

"No, not for her," she replied.

She didn't know who had moved, but now there

was no room between them. Shekita's breasts pressed against Pola's. She ached to remove their clothes where she could feel Pola's skin on hers.

"What do you want, Shekita?" Pola's head had lowered.

Their lips were millimeters away from each other. Her warm breath caressed Shekita's lips.

Shekita chose that moment to accept everything.

Pola was her bear, and she was hers.

"I want you to claim me," she whispered.

Pola's mouth came crashing down on hers. Shekita's eyes fluttered shut. She wrapped her arms around Pola's neck, holding on for dear life. Pola dominated the kiss, sending her tongue past Shekita's parted lips. Shekita met the kiss with the same fiery passion.

She didn't feel an ounce of regret over her decision. She loved everything about Pola. She wanted to show her how much she wanted her and needed her.

Pola tore her mouth from Shekita's. She pressed Shekita back against the door trailing hot, open-mouthed kisses along her jaw and down her neck. Shekita tilted her head to the side to grant Pola access.

While Pola took her time bathing Shekita's neck with her tongue, Shekita slipped her hands down to the tie that kept the robe closed. She wanted to see Pola's creamy skin, her high breasts, and light-brown nipples. Once it was undone, Shekita pushed the offending material off Pola's shoulders. It sailed down to the floor.

"Your turn," Pola ground out through clenched teeth.

She reached up and shredded Shekita's clothing with a partially shifted hand. Her talons were large, and her clothes were no match for them. Shekita watched in amazement how her hand shifted back to her human form. Pola assisted Shekita in brushing the tattered remains of her clothing to the floor, leaving her completely naked.

Their lips met in a scorching-hot kiss. Their tongues dueled together, their hands roaming each other's bodies. Pola's hands slid up her body until they cupped Shekita's cheeks.

"Do you know what you are asking of me?" Pola murmured. Her amber eyes glowed with an intense heat. Her warm body pressed close to Shekita's.

There was nothing else on Shekita's mind but to become the mate of this woman before her.

"I've waited my entire life for fate to present the perfect person for me. There are no mistakes when we believe. You are my mate, and I will protect you and love you with everything that I have."

The final barriers around Shekita's heart fell away. Those were words that she had longed to hear, and coming from Pola, she knew she could trust what she said. She was taking that leap of faith, and Pola would catch her.

Shekita bit her lip and nodded. She rested her hands on Pola's, a small smile forming on her lips.

"I'm yours. Claim me," she whispered.

Pola swooped down, capturing her lips again. This time the kiss was sweet and slow. There was no doubt in Shekita's mind that Pola cared for her. She sighed, leaning into her. Their bodies fit perfectly together. Pola's warm hands drifted over her body. Shekita gasped when her fingers arrived at her slit. Her finger pushed along, tracing Shekita's slick folds, slipping inside and connecting with her clit.

Shekita groaned, tearing her lips away from Pola's. She leaned back against the door, widening her legs. Pola took advantage of the move and rolled her sensitive flesh between her fingers.

"You like that?" Pola breathed. She leaned her

head down and nuzzled her face in the crook of Shekita's neck.

Shekita whimpered, unable to answer her. The sensation of Pola's fingers playing with her bundle of nerves was enough to send a ripple of desire through her.

Pola licked her neck, then grazed the same spot with her fangs. "I didn't hear you, mate."

"Yes," Shekita hissed. She arched her back, her breasts brushing Pola's soft skin. "Please, Pola."

Pola grunted, reaching down, and picked Shekita up by the backs of her thighs. Shekita immediately wrapped her legs around her as her bear walked them over to the couch. Shekita had never considered herself a petite woman, but the way that Pola handled her had her feeling small and cherished.

Her back met the soft cushions of the couch. Pola's body covered hers. She widened her legs to allow Pola to rest comfortably in the valley of her thighs. Pola's hand slipped between them and returned to her clit. Pola dipped her fingers inside Shekita's hot core. Her muscles clenched around the invading fingers.

Shekita thrust her hips toward Pola's hand, taking her fingers deep inside her. The need to reach an orgasm was growing. Her fingers pounded inside Shekita, filling her.

"Mine," Pola growled. Her fangs were brandished, her gaze hot as she watched Shekita. Her thumb came to rest on Shekita's clit, applying pressure, her fingers continuing to sink into her.

Everything disappeared from around them. Pola only saw her mate. The woman who had just promised everything she had ever wanted.

Nothing else mattered.

Pola knelt with one leg on the couch and the other on the floor. She focused on bringing immense amounts of pleasure to Shekita. Her other hand came to rest on Shekita's breast. Her hand molded to the fullness of Shekita's mound. She massaged and played with Shekita's breasts. Her fingers teased and tugged on her nipple, sending an electric current to Shekita's pussy.

This was more than Shekita could handle. Her hands flew out, and she gripped the cushions of the couch. The waves of her orgasm were sailing high, the sensation building until it broke.

Shekita screamed as she reached fulfillment. It was then that Pola bent down, her fangs sinking deep into the meat of Shekita's shoulder. The brief explosion of pain was immediately replaced with pleasure. Shekita tried to draw in a ragged gasp of air, but the sensations coursing through her body took her breath away.

There was nothing in Shekita's existence at the moment but Pola. Her warmth covered Shekita while she claimed her. Stars danced behind Shekita's eyelids, and she squeezed them tight. It was as if she were having an out-of-body experience. She had never had an orgasm this hard before. Her muscles relaxed, and she melted onto the couch. Pola's fingers were still lodged in her, and she carefully lifted her head from Shekita's. Her warm tongue bathed the tender area.

Shekita was finally able to breathe again. She inhaled quickly, and small tendrils of arousal returned. There was something about Pola bathing her neck with her tongue that caused her core to tingle. Her pussy gushed with the proof of her desire. Pola slowly moved her fingers again, thrusting them in and out of Shekita's drenched channel.

Shekita opened her eyes and took in the site of Pola's lips, slick with her blood and her own saliva. She licked her lips, and Shekita's body trembled. She reached up and took Shekita's legs and turned her around on the couch to where she knelt between Shekita's legs. She yanked on Shekita, bringing her ass to the edge of the couch and eased her legs up and out of the way.

Shekita's breath caught in her throat as she watched Pola's head descend between her legs. The second Pola's mouth covered her pussy, she cried out.

Shekita teetered on the edge of another climax. Her hand shot out and rested on the back of Pola's head while she feasted on her. Shekita's breaths turned into pants. Pola's expert tongue pushed her even closer to her next release.

"Pola," she chanted.

Her hips moved like they had a mind of their own. Shekita became wanton, using both hands to hold Pola to her. She would take all of the pleasure this woman wanted to give her. She glanced down and moaned, watching Pola hold her labia open while she suckled on her swollen bundle.

She slid her two fingers back inside Shekita and continued to use her tongue to please her.

There was nothing Shekita could do but lie back and allow her mate to consume her. She tightened her hold on Pola's hair and kept her legs out of the way. Tears escaped from her eyes at the realization that in just a short period of time, she had fallen in love with Pola.

Why she had ever fought this, she didn't know. From the moment they'd met, she'd known Pola was nothing like Bobbie.

Shekita's cries filled the air. Pola continued to sensually assault her until a shudder racked through Shekita's body. She gripped Pola's hair tight, the waves of her next orgasm washing over her. She screamed, her release exploding from her. Spasms ripped through her, and she rode the current of her climax. She fell back against the couch, her skin coated with sweat, her thighs dripping with her release.

Pola lifted her head, her face coated with Shekita's juices. She smiled a cocky grin.

"My mate," she murmured. Her fingers were still lodged within Shekita. She leaned over her, resting a hand on the couch.

Shekita guided her head down and offered her lips to her.

She tasted herself on Pola's tongue. The kiss grew deep and frantic. A blossom of heat burgeoned from the depths of Shekita's stomach. She didn't know what it was, but she felt as if her body were on fire.

Pola pulled back slightly. Her eyes, bright with desire, stared at her. Shekita whimpered her complaint at the feeling of Pola withdrawing her fingers from her. She held up her drenched hand and eyed the creamy nectar that coated them.

"You taste as sweet as honey," Pola murmured.

She suckled on a finger in her mouth, a low-pitched growl emanating from her. She brought the other one to Shekita who didn't hesitate to part her lips. She tasted Pola's fingers, holding her wrist, and cleaned every single finger.

Her core pulsed. Her body was aflame. She had the deep craving for her mate and more of the pleasure she could provide.

"What is wrong with me?" Shekita whispered. "Why do I need you so? And why do I feel as if I'm on fire?"

Pola grinned and leaned down, drawing her tongue around Shekita's perky nipple. She nipped it with her teeth, inciting a shiver through Shekita.

"It's the mating fever, my love." She stood from the floor and easily lifted Shekita from the couch as if she weighed no more than a pillow.

Shekita wrapped her legs around her mate as she walked through her house.

"Where's the bedroom?" Pola asked.

Shekita pointed to the closed doorway at the end of the hallway. "Mating fever?"

"Oh, yes, mate."

Pola arrived at the door and kicked it open with her foot. She made her way to Shekita's bed and gently deposited her on the middle of it. The lamp on the bedside table had been left on, allowing Shekita to see the flames of desire in Pola's eyes.

"You and I will spend plenty of time pleasuring each other until we can no longer move," Pola said.

She climbed over Shekita, but it was Shekita who flipped them to where she was on top. She rested her hands on Pola's wrists, trapping them against the bed. She smiled, welcoming the tantalizing sensations that were coursing through her body. Desire, lust, and need grew inside her. The mating mark that Pola had bestowed upon her barely hurt.

With the knowledge that she belonged to Pola, it fed all of those emotions swirling around in her. Pola had given her not one but two orgasms in the living room, and now it was time for her to return the favor.

"Well, if that is the case, then allow me to have my fill of you next."

CHAPTER ELEVEN

Five days of wonderful bliss. Pola grinned at the thought of how many days she had stayed wrapped up in the arms of the woman she loved. It had taken everything she had to finally leave her home.

She had missed so many phone calls and text messages while she had been locked away with Shekita. Once their mating fever had died down, they'd come back to reality. The fever could last up to a week. Pola grinned thinking of how well she and Shekita had come to know each other.

It had taken Pola two hours to return all of the calls and text messages that had been waiting for her. She had to assure her family she was safe. Her mother had been close to hysterics when she had come onto the phone. It was rare for them not to speak daily, and she had alerted the enforcers that Pola had been missing. It had been Saffron who'd figured it out, calmed Theola down, and canceled the soon-to-be manhunt.

The moment she had mentioned the word *mate* and confirmed that indeed she was safe and had sealed the bond, the conversation had changed. Her mother had turned to demanding she bring Shekita over immediately so they may meet her.

Pola sighed and stared out the small window of the office. She would love nothing but to be still wrapped up in her mate's arms, locked away together, but unfortunately, they had bills that needed to be paid, and that would require that they returned to work. She stood by the copier while it processed the job she was waiting for. Her bear longed to see Shekita again. After work, they had plans to go to the Pride home for dinner.

Her bear whined, pacing back and forth inside her chest.

"You'll be fine. We get off work in one hour," she grumbled.

"Talking to yourself?" Eddie's voice sounded behind her.

Pola swung around, having not heard the alpha approach her. She relaxed and smiled sheepishly.

"Actually, my bear. She wasn't too happy we had to leave our mate." Pola stood taller at the mention of Shekita.

"The offer for another week off still stands," Eddie replied. The alpha had been very accommodating about her missed workdays. A mating for a bear shifter was intense and required time for the bond to solidify. When Saffron and Dasha had mated, their fever had lasted about the same as Pola and Shekita's. "Take some time off. This work will still be here."

"I shouldn't At least not now. I'd prefer to take some time once we decide on living arrangements and stuff." There were a lot of decisions they had to make, but Pola wasn't worried about it. They would figure it out. They had a lifetime to do so.

"I'm happy for you, Pola. You deserve to find someone to spend your life with."

Eddie smiled softly, and it piqued Pola's curiosity. Something fleeting appeared in Eddie's eyes then was gone. Had the alpha found love at one point in her life?

Both she and the beta were unmated. It led for some tensions around the clan because she hadn't taken a mate yet. Her line hadn't been secured and wouldn't be until she had an heir. There had even been a few challenges for her seat as alpha, but Eddie was a strong bear and had bested both men who'd thought they were better. It had been years since someone had stepped forward to challenge her.

"Thanks, Alpha." The copier screeched a noise. Pola glanced at it and saw that it was out of paper. She reached for a bundle sitting on the shelves next to it. She glanced back over at the alpha while loading the machine. She doubted the woman had come over to check on her for talking aloud to herself. "Was there something you needed?"

"Actually, yes. I almost forgot what I came over here for." Eddie stepped forward, holding out a thick, sealed manilla envelope.

Pola glanced down at it and saw the emblem for Harper Construction.

"The contract for all of the renovations has been signed," Eddie said. "I figured you could leave a little early and drop this off to your mate. She can give it to her brother when she goes to their office."

"Yes, ma'am." Pola's lips spread into a wide grin.

"Get out of here." Eddie tossed her a wink and spun on her heel and walked away.

Pola couldn't contain her excitement. She finished up the job she was working on and flew around her office gathering her belongings. The Lick and Bite wasn't that far from her job. She wouldn't mind hanging out with Shekita while she finished up. Their plan had been for them to run to Pola's place after work, get cleaned up, and then head to the Prime home for dinner.

Pola was so excited to introduce her mate to her family.

Once in her car, she had to lay off the gas so hard. It wouldn't do her any good to get pulled over and get a ticket. She rolled the windows down and allowed the air to flow through her vehicle. The music was blasting, and she was singing along with it.

Her life was perfect.

She arrived at the Lick and Bite and couldn't find a parking spot near it. She drove a little farther down the road and finally found somewhere to park. It was a lovely day, and she wouldn't mind the small walk. She had been in the office all day, and it would do her some good to stretch her legs out.

Grabbing the envelope she was to deliver, she locked up her car and began her trek along the sidewalk. The sun's warm rays shined down, caressing her skin. She'd worn a calf-length sundress with sandals. Her bare arms soaked up the sun.

"Hey, Pola!" a familiar voice shouted.

She glanced across the street. Nick and Sega stood on the corner.

"Hey, guys!" She waved to them. They were two of the enforcers for their clan. She paused her walk at the sight of them jogging across the street toward her. "How's it going?"

"That's what we are coming to ask you." Nick laughed.

"We hear congratulations are in order," Sega's deep voice boomed. He slapped her on the shoulder, and she jerked forward from his strength. Sometimes her bigger male counterparts forgot how strong they were.

"Thank you." Pola was sure there was a wide, silly grin on her face. She collapsed the envelope to her chest in her folded arms.

"We are having a party, right?" Nick asked.

"I'm not sure, but that would be fun. We haven't

had a good ol'-fashioned mating reception in a while," Pola mused. Her sister hadn't wanted one. She was too much of an introvert and private. Saffron hadn't minded.

It could be fun.

"You know what, I'll mention it to my mate and see what she says." Pola added this to her growing list of things that she and Shekita needed to discuss.

"I can't wait to meet your mate. Don't be shy. Bring her around," Sega said.

"I will." She offered them a wave and continued her journey. Her bear was quite anxious to see their mate again. Pola put a little more pep in her step and hurried to the ice cream shop.

She arrived and swung open the door. As always, the music was blaring when she stepped foot inside. The construction crew were working on the final details. Tables and chairs were positioned around the establishment. The countertops sparkled, and the artwork on the walls was bright and welcoming. There were a few standing refrigerators that would allow patrons to come and purchase prepackaged ice cream and other frozen desserts.

Pola grew excited for her friend. The reopening of the Lick and Bite would be epic.

A tall man with a baseball cap came from out the back. A work belt lined with tools rested low on his waist.

"Can I help—oh, aren't you Shekita's mate?" He offered her a wide grin. He walked from behind the purchase counter.

"I am," Pola responded. Pride filled her at the thought of her mate mentioning her. She couldn't wait to go around introducing her mate to everyone she knew. Maybe they should think of having a party. She was sure her mother would love that idea.

"I'm Ryan." He held his hand out for her.

She took his in a firm handshake.

"She's been talking about you all day," he said.

"Is that so?" Pola's cheeks were hurting from all of her grinning. She inhaled, picking up on her mate's scent. It was fleeting and not as strong as it should be if she were there. "Where is she?"

"She left to run to the hardware store. She should have been back by now." He took his cap off and raked his fingers through his hair before replacing it.

Pola laughed. Her mate was nervous about meeting her family. Maybe she had stopped to pick up a gift for her parents. She had been inquiring on what they liked and that she didn't want to arrive at their home empty-handed.

"You mind if I leave this here? I'm going to see if I can find her." Pola waved the envelope in the air.

"Not at all. Just drop it on the counter."

"Thanks!" She spun around and placed it down then rushed out the door. There were plenty of shops in between the hardware store and the Lick and Bite. She lifted her chin and breathed in. She'd follow her nose to find her mate.

"You have such a glow to you," the cashier mentioned.

Shekita took her change and receipt and slid it into her jeans pocket. She had left Ryan at the shop alone so she could run and get a few things. She didn't know how she didn't have handles for the cabinets behind the checkout counter. Thankfully, there was a hardware store within walking distance from the shop. Today she had let the other guys leave early since they were now putting the finishing touches on the project. Ryan had volunteered to do last-minute cleaning while she ran for the simple items they needed.

"Why thank you, but I don't think I have a glow to me." She chuckled.

The older woman's smooth brown skin was marred by the wrinkles surrounding her eyes and her mouth. Her salt-and-pepper hair was pulled back away from her face in a bun. She was one who smiled and laughed often.

"Oh, you most certainly do have a glow to you." The cashier's tag displayed the name: Linda. She held a twinkle in her eyes, leaned on the counter, and rested her chin in her hand. "You look like someone who is in love."

Was she that obvious?

She must be.

That morning when she'd arrived at the shop, the guys had noticed something different, too. They couldn't put their finger on it. They'd hounded her until she had to come clean on where she had been. She shared with them that not only did she meet someone, but that she was a bear shifter and they were fated mates.

She would have never thought she would be in a relationship again. Bobbie had taught her a valuable lesson. One that she would always hold near and dear to her heart.

Love doesn't hurt.

"You can tell that just by looking at me?" Shekita tried to hold back her grin, but it broke through. She couldn't remember a time where she was so happy. Tonight she would get to meet Pola's family. Butterflies already filled her stomach at the thought of meeting her new in-laws. Even though Pola had assured her they would love her and wouldn't care that she was human, Shekita was worried.

"I sure can." Linda smirked. "Go ahead and tell me I'm right. You, my dear, are in love."

Linda slapped the counter and barked a hefty laugh. Shekita rolled her eyes, a giggle escaping her. She couldn't lie to the lady.

"Maybe I am," she teased.

Linda's laughter grew. Shekita couldn't help but join her. Linda's good nature and laughter were infectious.

"Well, anyone who puts a smile like that on your face is a keeper. You have a wonderful day, my dear," Linda said.

"Thanks, you, too." Shekita hefted up the bag and gave the woman a wave, leaving the store.

Breathing in the fresh air, she couldn't help but remain in her good mood. There were a few stores she wanted to sneak into before returning back to the Lick And Bite. She wanted to find Mrs. Prime a gift.

Shekita strolled down the main road, oblivious to her surroundings. She was floating on cloud nine while window shopping. She stopped in front of a home goods store and took in the display behind the glass. She pressed her nose to it and decided she'd go inside. There was a nice vase that caught her eye, and she thought it would be perfect for Mrs. Prime. Stepping back, she spun around and froze in place.

Bobbie stood ten feet from her.

"You've ignored my phone calls and text messages," Bobbie said. She was dressed in her signature jeans, sleeveless tank top, and boots.

Shekita inhaled sharply. After her appearance at her home, she had blocked Bobbie's number.

Shekita had hoped that Bobbie would just leave her alone, but apparently, Bobbie was still the same old possessive woman.

You're not going to have your fucking bodyguard around at all times, Shekita.

Shekita swallowed hard. She glanced around

and took in people minding their own business, cars driving by. Bobbie wouldn't try anything crazy in public.

Would she?

"There is nothing for us to say. I've moved on," Shekita replied, finally finding her voice. She tightened her grip on her bag and took a step away from Bobbie.

"You don't get to just ignore me. You think you've moved on, but I told you that you will always belong to me." Bobbie strode forward and gripped her arm.

Shekita winced and tried to pull away.

"Let me go," Shekita demanded. Panic set in, her voice rising.

A few people strolling along the sidewalk on the other side of the street looked their way. Humiliation set in at the thought of someone witnessing her and Bobbie. In the past, Bobbie would only be cruel when they were alone, never in public where people would see. She always created a persona that she was a kind and fun person, when in reality, she was far from it.

Bobbie yanked her harder, and Shekita fell into her. Shekita inhaled and gagged slightly. The stench of alcohol poured from Bobbie's lips.

She had been drinking.

"You are coming back home with me. I am done with your nonsense. You've had your little fun." Her nails dug into the meat of Shekita's arm. She practically dragged Shekita over to where her car was parked.

"I'm not going anywhere with you." Shekita struggled to free herself from the hard grip.

They were drawing an audience from pedestrians in the area. No one spoke or said anything, so she did something she'd never done before. Opened her mouth and screamed, "Help!"

CHAPTER TWELVE

The blood in Pola's veins chilled at the sound of a scream for help. She paused at the corner of the street and glanced to her right where the scream had come from. She knew that voice. It was her mate, and she was in trouble.

Her gaze landed on a very familiar figure struggling to break free from an assailant.

The beast in her roared, slamming her head against Pola's chest.

Mate! In danger, her bear growled.

Pola took off running toward them. Her feet ate up the pavement, her shifter genes lending her strength to allow her to move faster than the average woman.

"Get your hands off her," Pola growled.

Bobbie had Shekita pressed against her car, trying to get the passenger door open.

"This is none of your business," Bobbie snapped. She looked over her shoulder at Pola. "This is between me and Shekita."

"That is my mate you have your hands on. I'm going to tell you one more time. Get off of her," Pola warned.

"Or what?" Bobbie challenged. She spun around to face Pola and took a step toward her. "Am I supposed to be afraid of you, bear?"

"Come here, Shekita." Pola motioned for her to move beside her, but Bobbie's arm blocked her path. She snagged Shekita's arm, coaxing another growl from Pola. Her bear was not happy to see another woman's hand on her mate. This was a person who had hurt their lover, and her bear was not going to stand for it any longer.

"She's not yours. She was mine first."

"And I left you," Shekita snapped. She tugged, dropping a bag she held. She yanked harder until she broke free and rushed over to Pola who pushed her behind her.

"Don't ever think about my mate. Don't contact her, and if I ever see you touching her again—"

"You'll what?" Bobbie pulled small pocketknife from her jeans. She flipped it open, revealing the weapon.

Pola wasn't worried about it. Shekita was behind her and safe.

"You don't want to know," Pola barked.

"Oh, I think I do. Shekita will never be yours. She was mine first, and I'll keep coming for her."

Pola gave a roar and dashed forward. She barreled into Bobbie. The need to protect Shekita overcame her. Shekita carried her mark. The bear in her demanded they prove that to the world.

They fell against Bobbie's vehicle. Pola gripped Bobbie's wrist tight and slammed it against the truck. She repeated the motion, trying to get her to drop the knife. There was an audience gathering near them. Pola ignored them, her focus on the person who'd dared to hurt her mate.

Bobbie swung her other arm, landing a punch to the side of Pola's head. A gasp escaped Pola. She inhaled and squeezed Bobbie's wrist, raising her other hand to ward off the blows that Bobbie kept landing on her.

"Stay away from Shekita," Pola ground out

through clenched teeth. She was fighting her bear who was demanding to break free. Her animal was going frantic inside her. She wanted to break free to teach Bobbie a lesson, but the human would be no match for a pissed-off grizzly bear.

"She's mine." Bobbie laughed.

She brought her knee up, but Pola was quicker, turning away. The knee landed on the outer part of her thigh.

"Do you think she would really want someone like you? A shifter?"

Bobbie used her knee, and this time, Pola didn't block her. Pain exploded between Pola's legs. She gasped, letting go of Bobbie's wrist. She staggered backward, inhaling sharply. The pain was over-whelming but fading fast.

"I do want her," Shekita snapped. She raced to Pola's side and slipped an arm around her waist.

Pola stood to her full height and wrapped an arm around her shoulder and turned. She wasn't much of a fighter in her human form. As long as her mate was safe, that was all that mattered.

"Leave us be."

Pola swiveled Shekita around and took a few steps away, crying out.

A burning sensation sank deep into the muscle

of her shoulder. She spun around, fear escaping her.

The crazed woman had sunk her knife into Pola's shoulder blade.

"Don't turn your back on me!" Bobbie hollered. "Fight me like a woman."

Pola's bear no longer took no for an answer. Her fangs pushed forth through her gums and descended. Her dark-brown fur sprouted out onto her flesh. Her bear broke free. Her clothes fell to the ground in a pile of tattered remains. The knife that was once in her shoulder landed on the sidewalk.

Shekita reversed, and the scent of fear permeated the air.

Pola stood to her full height and threw her head back and let loose a mighty roar.

The thought that her mate was afraid of her pissed off her animal even more. If the dumb bitch had just left them alone, she wouldn't have had to shift into her bear to protect her woman. She inhaled again and this time she noticed that the stink of fear she was scenting was not that of her mate. Shekita's eyes were wide as she stepped away. Pola swung around and faced Bobbie who stood before her with her mouth agape.

"Holy shit," Bobbie muttered. Her body jerked into movement as if she were just regaining control of it. She backed off with her palms up, facing Pola. "You can have her."

Pola fell to all fours, baring her fangs. Screams went around from the pedestrians trying to get to safety. The scene turned into a melee. Men, women, and children were now running. The screeching of tires filled the air. Pola was sure she made one hell of a sight. It wasn't often there was a bear in the middle of a busy shopping district.

So it had taken her shifting for this idiot of a woman to get that she needed to leave Shekita alone.

"I'll walk away from her. You can have the bitch," Bobbie said.

Pola advanced on her, following her as she scrambled around her truck. The color escaped her face, leaving her pale.

"Pola! No!" a deep male voice shouted from behind her, but her bear ignored it.

The lowlife before her had hurt her woman. She didn't deserve to walk off. Pola's bear was pushing for full control.

It was taking everything Pola had to keep some form of control between the two of them. Usually, she stayed in control even when in bear form, but at the moment, her bear was furious. She wanted to exact revenge for all of the times Bobbie had hurt their mate.

During their five days of being locked indoors with each other during their fever, Shekita had come clean about Bobbie. She'd shared everything about her prior relationship with this female, and most of it was not good. This woman had hurt their mate. Physically and mentally. She didn't deserve to even look at Shekita.

"Pola! Stop." A male threw himself in front of her.

She blinked and took in Nick glaring at her. She reached out a hand and held her gaze. She brandished her fangs. Her bear recognized him but didn't want to harm him. He wasn't her target.

"Don't do this," he said.

The sound of sirens echoed around them. Pola took in the arrival of the human police. The cops flew out of their cars, brandishing their weapons.

"Don't shoot her!" Shekita raced forward and dove in front of her.

Pola snarled at the thought of her mate in the line of fire from the police. If the police shot her, the bullets wouldn't do anything but piss her bear off even more.

"That woman stabbed her in the back, causing her to shift in self-defense!"

Shekita pointed to Bobbie who spun on her heel and tried to make a break for it. Sega's swift form raced after her. She was no match for a shifter's speed. He tackled her down onto the ground.

"I'm a Brown Claw enforcer, and I will take full responsibility for Pola Pride shifting. But someone better damn well arrest that woman for assaulting a member of my clan," Nick stated. He joined Shekita in standing in front of Pola.

She huffed, not wanting to be protected. She was a mighty bear and could take care of herself.

The police put away their weapons.

"Nick, get her to shift back to her human form," one of the officers said. He motioned for two of his men to go over to where Sega was kneeling on the back of Bobbie. "Someone better tell me what the hell is going on."

Nick spun around and leveled Pola with a hard glare.

"Shift back, Pola. Now."

Pola returned his stare, not intimidated by him in the least, but it was Shekita's soft touch that got her attention. Her mate stood close, resting a hand on the side of Pola's fur-covered face.

"Give me back my Pola," she said gently.

Pola leaned into her hand. Her bear loved the feeling of their mate's hand on her fur. She nuzzled Shekita's hand, feeling herself soften. Her bear was a sucker for their mate.

Anything Shekita wanted, it was hers.

Pola's bear released a whine.

"Please?" Shekita whispered.

Pola locked eyes with her mate's big brown ones. Immediately, her bear turned the reins over to her. Pola grabbed a hold of them and pushed forward, taking back control of their body. The fur that lined her receded. Her bones shifted and short-ened back into the human form. Within seconds, she was back to herself, kneeling on the hard concrete.

Pola grimaced at the bite of the ground on her bare knees.

"You're back," Shekita exclaimed. She helped Pola to her feet.

"Can we get a blanket for her," the same cop shouted over his shoulder. He walked forward and stopped before them.

One of the younger officers jogged over to them with a dark blanket in his hand.

Pola murmured her thanks and took it. She wrapped it around herself, toga style. Unable to resist, she took Shekita's hand in hers.

"I'm Officer Brady. What is going on here?" he asked.

"That woman was over there assaulting my mate. She was trying to take her," Pola's voice ended on a growl.

The cop's eyes narrowed on her. Shekita ran her fingers along the inner part of her arm softly.

"It's okay," Shekita murmured, glancing up at her.

"Are you good, Pola?" Nick asked. As an enforcer, he had the power to arrest her.

She swallowed hard, not wanting to cause any more trouble.

"Yes, I'm fine." It would be hard to explain to her alpha that she had lost control and had to be arrested.

"Is what she said true, ma'am?" Officer Brady asked Shekita.

"Yes. Bobbie Curtis and I have a history together. She was trying to force me against my will to get into her car. Pola came to my rescue." Shekita paused, big fat tears spilling down her face.

Pola wrapped an arm around her. She glanced over Office Brady's shoulder. Other police officers placed Bobbie in handcuffs. A few other spectators must have come back. Two women were standing near them speaking with the cops.

"It's okay, my love," Pola murmured. She pressed a kiss to Shekita's forehead and gave her another squeeze.

"But is your shoulder all right? I keep seeing the knife sticking out of it," Shekita said. She reached up and wiped her cheeks with the back of her hand.

"I'm good as new with my shift." Pola rotated her shoulder and only felt a twinge of pain. It would be completely gone by morning.

"I'll need the both of you to meet us down at the station for an official statement," Officer Brady said. He turned to Nick. "I'm sure you will want to be present for this."

"Of course. All members of the clan must be accompanied by an enforcer or clan leaders," Nick said. He took Officer Brady's hand in a firm shake.

The officer nodded to Shekita and Pola, walking away.

Once he was out of earshot, Nick turned to them. "Are you sure she didn't hurt you?"

"The knife didn't go that far in." Pola shrugged.

Sega returned to them, joining in the conversation. "That woman is crazy." He shook his head. He towered over all of them. It was a wonder someone his size could move as fast as he could. "We need to go down to the police station?"

"Yeah. The girls will need to go down there to give a statement," Nick shared.

"Will I have time to run and get some clothes? I don't have anything extra with me," Pola asked. As a shifter, she didn't have a problem walking around naked, but humans always had issues with naked shifters.

"We'll escort you home and then down to the station," Nick said.

"I'll alert the alpha to what is going on." Sega pulled his phone from his jeans and stepped away.

"Stay here. I'll go get my truck, and we'll ride together." Nick backed away, turned on his heel, and jogged down the street.

Pola blew out a deep breath and faced her mate. She reached up and cupped Shekita's face.

"She didn't hurt you, did she?" Pola asked.

"No, you came just in time." Shekita's eyes watered again with unshed tears. She rested her hand on Pola's. A small smile appeared on her lips. "I love you so much."

Pola's heart stuttered. She froze, unsure she'd heard her mate correctly.

"What did you say?" she asked softly.

"I love you, Pola Pride. I was going to tell you later, but now seemed the best time to do it. My heart beats for you, and there is no other person I would rather be with in this world but you."

"Oh, I love you, too," Pola breathed. She gathered Shekita to her and wrapped her up tight in her embrace. She had searched her entire life for the person who she would share her life with. The fates knew exactly who she needed in her life, and they never made mistakes. Shekita was perfect for her. "I will always be here to protect you and love you."

Neither of them paid attention to the craziness that was going on around them. Pola had eyes for only Shekita. This woman was her entire world, and she would go up against one thousand Bobbies to keep Shekita safe. Her bear snorted in agreement.

Shekita belonged to her and her bear.

Fate had given this woman to her, and she had claimed her.

No one would ever take her away.

EPILOGUE

Shekita stretched her limbs out as far as they could reach. She sighed, loving the feeling of the warmth of the sun. She and her mate were enjoying their beautiful Saturday afternoon. Shekita had packed them a nice lunch, and they had set off into the woods so Pola could let her bear out. Shekita might have overdone it on the food, but she didn't care. They could take the rest home and have it for dinner later.

While her mate was off doing her bear thing, she had planned to read a good book. She had picked up a new thriller from the local bookstore.

Shekita rolled over onto her stomach and opened the book.

Life couldn't get any better.

It had been three months since the altercation with Bobbie. She had been arrested and charged with assault with a deadly weapon. She was currently awaiting her trial in a jail cell. There was enough evidence stacked against her. It was going to be a long time before she breathed an ounce of freedom.

Shekita inhaled the wonderful scent of nature that surrounded her. She was no longer going to allow Bobbie to inch into her thoughts any longer. She had a bright and loving future ahead of her.

With her book open, she lost herself in this mesmerizing tale. This was what she needed. Fresh air, good food, and a relaxing book. Her lips curved up into a smile. Everything between Shekita and Pola was perfect. They had come to the decision to have her move into Pola's home. It was bigger, and they enjoyed immense privacy on her property. They had even spoken about expanding and renovating the house. Shekita would, of course, be in charge of that. She wanted to make the cabin a home they would be able to grow their family.

She had lost track of time, and soon, the sounds

of a big animal crashing through the woods greeted her. She lifted her head in time to see a familiar brown grizzly flying out of the tree line. Shekita laughed at Pola's antics.

The large bear slowed down and ambled over to her. Shekita slid her bookmark into the book then set it aside. She pushed up into a sitting position and watched her bear. The love that swelled in her heart for this bear took her breath away.

"You're back," Shekita murmured.

Pola grunted, then arrived in front of her. She nuzzled Shekita's neck with her snout. Shekita laughed, wrapping her arms around Pola's thick neck. Pola bumped her with her head, sending Shekita sprawling onto her back. The air around Pola shimmered. Shekita lifted onto her elbows, waiting for her mate to shift back into her human form.

Within moments, a very naked Pola knelt on the soft, thick grass. Her amber eyes were filled with heat, and she gazed upon Shekita.

"I told you I wasn't going far," Pola murmured. She slowly crawled to Shekita until she was braced over her.

Shekita fell back onto the ground, eyeing her mate. She immediately felt her body become aroused. It was a never-ending reaction when her mate was close to her.

She never could get enough of Pola.

"I missed you while you were gone," Shekita admitted softly.

Pola leaned down and captured her lips in a slow, passionate kiss. The heat between them burned even brighter. Shekita's body grew flush as Pola's tongue stroked hers. She reached up and wrapped her arms around Pola and drew her down to lie on top of her.

"You never have to worry. I will always return to you," Pola murmured. Her lips brushed Shekita's again. She pressed her face into the crook of Shekita's neck. "I love you, and you belong to me."

"That I do, babe," Shekita breathed.

Pola lifted her head again, and they stared into each other's eyes. There was no other place Shekita would rather be. She had found the love of her life, and she was going to hold on to her forever.

ABOUT THE AUTHOR

Ariel Marie is an author who loves the paranormal, action and hot steamy romance. She combines all three in each and every one of her stories. For as long as she can remember, she has loved vampires, shifters and every creature you can think of. This even rolls over into her favorite movies. She loves a good action packed thriller! Throw a touch of the supernatural world in it and she's hooked!

Sign up for Ariel Marie's newsletter!
Scan the QR Code to get all the latest news from Ariel
Marie!

For more information visit:
www.thearielmarie.com

The Nightstar Shifters

No wolf can resist the call to mate.

Strong female wolves are in search of their mate. The desire is strong for these women who long to find the one person meant for them.

They are fierce and determined, putting their trust in fate.

If you love lesbian wolf shifter romance filled with action and adventure, then you will love the Nightstar Shifters series.

Ready to start the Nightstar Shifters? Click HERE to download book one!

Vampires and Humans. Are they meant to be together? One drop of blood will control their futures.

After the war between vampires and humankind, Earth was never the same. This new world was dangerous, and vampires were on the hunt for their fated mates. The installation of the draft should have made things simpler, but all it did was create chaos.

Humans didn't want to conform to the new ways of life.

Vampires had no problems making them.

Enter this new dark and sexy world full of lesbian vampire romance. The Immortal Reign series is an adult-themed paranormal romance that you will want to sink your teeth into. If you love action-packed, sizzling hot wlw romances, then this is the series for you.

Start the Immortal Reign series today! Click HERE to download book one!

ALSO BY ARIEL MARIE

<u>The Montana Grizzlies</u>

Hot For Her Bear

Claimed by Her Bear

Bound to Her Bear

Marked by Her Bear

<u>The Nightstar Shifters</u>

Sailing With Her Wolf

Protecting Her Wolf

Sealed With A Bite

Hers to Claim

Wanted by the Wolf

Taming Her Mate

<u>The Immortal Reign series</u>

Deadly Kiss

Iced Heart

Royal Bite

Wicked Allure

<u>Blackclaw Alphas (Reverse Harem Series)</u>

Fate of Four

Bearing Her Fate (TBD)

<u>The Midnight Coven Brand</u>

Forever Desired

Wicked Shadows

<u>Paranormal Erotic Box Sets</u>

Vampire Destiny (An Erotic Vampire Box Set)

Moon Valley Shifters Box Set (F/F Shifters)

The Dragon Curse Series (Ménage MFF Erotic Series)

<u>The Dark Shadows Series</u>

Princess

Toma

Phaelyn

Teague

Adrian

Nicu

<u>Stand Alone Books</u>

Dani's Return

A Faery's Kiss

Tiger Haven

Searching For His Mate

A Tiger's Gift

Stone Heart (The Gargoyle Protectors)

Saving Penny

A Beary Christmas

Howl for Me

Birthright

Return to Darkness

Red and the Alpha